MW01193201

CUFFED

JOANNA BLAKE

Contents

For Casey and Michelle who were gone too soon

NEWSLETTER SIGNUP

To learn more about my books, giveaways and more please sign up here!

No spam, ever!

Xoxox,

Joanna

CUFFED

I've got her under lock and key. It's against the law to take advantage of the situation. But I'm about to break all the rules, just to make her mine.

I'm a government agent assigned to take down a notorious biker gang. She's just a girl who was in the wrong place at the wrong time. But I can't bend the rules, even though I know she's innocent.

Casey Jones is a natural beauty with curves that won't quit. With her big doe eyes and long legs, she's pure temptation. She's barely old enough to be working in a place that serves alcohol, but I can't stop myself from wanting to make her a woman.

My woman.

She's in the middle of something bad and too stubborn to see it. She owes these guys for giving her a job when she ran away from home as a kid.

Now all I want to do is protect her.

STOP!

P lease do NOT go back to the beginning of this book before closing it. If you do, the book will not count as being read and the author will not be credited.

Please use the TOC (located in the upper left hand of your screen) to navigate this book. If you're zoomed out, please tap the center of the screen to ensure you are out of page flip mode.

This is true for all authors enrolled in Kindle Unlimited and as such, this message will appear in all of our books that are enrolled in Kindle Unlimited.

Thank you so much for understanding,

Pincushion Press

PROLOGUE

I stood on the street in the freezing rain, wondering if this was it. If I was going to end up sick or worse. In a ditch somewhere. I looked around for shelter but there was nothing.

There wasn't anywhere to go from here.

I'd been heading down the coast, keeping mostly to the service roads. I was hoping to find someplace warm to wait out the winter.

Or at least, warmer.

I'd barely gotten fifteen miles from my last foster home before the rain started.

Home. That was a laugh.

My scrawny arms wrapped around my torso as I crossed the road . I hurried down the sidewalk past rows of small, somewhat rundown houses. The kind of neighborhood that wasn't rich, but cared enough to plant a few flowers.

Or at least that's the impression I got through the freezing rain.

I'd gone half a block when a door opened. I heard a gravelly voice say 'hey kid." I was about to run when a huge wall of a man stepped into my path.

"You got someplace to go?"

I stared up at him, the rain washing over both of us. He stared right back at me, absolutely impervious to the water. I was squinting but he looked like he was actually challenging the rain.

Daring it to get him wet.

He was big and tall, with long dark hair and piercing eyes. He was dressed in denim and leather, though he didn't seem too worried about it getting ruined.

I should have run. I was thinking about it, though he could have easily stopped me. But one thing stood out to me. The most surprising thing you could notice about a giant man who looked like a norse god and a badass from a Quentin Tarantino movie rolled into one.

The giant had kind eyes.

I'm not sure why but I shook my head in answer to his question. No, I definitely did not have someplace to go.

"What's your name, kid?"

I chewed my lip, realizing I needed a new name.

"Casey." I lied. It was close enough to my real name. My old name. The one that didn't matter anymore. The name of a girl who'd had parents. And lost them.

Besides, I'd had a friend named Casey once.

The man considered me, and then nodded.

"Well, I guess you better come inside."

I hesitated.

"You a pervert?"

He laughed and shook his head.

"No, hon. I got a thing for strays is all."

I followed him to the side door of the house. It was hard to see much in the torrential downpour but it looked well kept. It definitely wasn't anything fancy.

I stepped inside the kitchen and the smell of home cooking hit me. My stomach growled so loudly that the big man heard it. He raised an eyebrow.

"That hungry, eh?"

A scruffy looking dog and two fat cats stared at me from different spots in the kitchen. I stood near the door in case I had to run for it. But for some reason, the animals put me at ease.

"Saw you out the window."

He ladled me out a bowl of stew and set in on the table. I shouldn't have eaten it but my body took over. I moved so fast you would have thought I was starving.

I *was* starving. And cold. And pissed off at the world.

But for the first time in months, I wasn't scared.

He sat across from me and opened a beer.

"Well, Casey, I'm Mason. And if you've got someplace you should be I'd surely like to hear about it."

I stopped eating for just long enough to answer him.

"No place to be."

He scratched his chin as I shoveled food into my face. Good food. Magically delicious food.

The broth was tomato-y but I tasted celery and onions and hmmm... potatoes.

"How old are you, kid?"

I glared at him a little.

"Not a kid. Fifteen."

He grinned at me.

"Is that so? My apologies young lady."

"Not a girl."

He laughed and shook his head.

"Whatever you say, Casey."

How the hell had he known I was a girl? I'd tucked all my hair into a baseball cap. And I was wearing every t-shirt I owned under a hooded sweatshirt and a denim jacket.

I was in disguise, dammit.

"You need a place to stay?"

I shrugged. I didn't want to seem too eager. But I would have killed for a place to stay. After a handful of days on the run, I'd realized finding a safe place to sleep was next to impossible.

You could doze with your back against a wall, but actual sleep? That was a joke.

"I guess."

"Well, I got a spare bedroom in the back."

I looked at him, desperate to believe he was just a nice, big, tattoo covered man.

"What's the catch?"

"No catch."

"Don't like charity. Don't need it."

"Fair enough. I got plenty of work for an enterprising young lady such as yourself."

I nodded. I didn't bother telling him I was a boy again. The jig was up.

"Deal."

He smiled at me as I held out my hand and shook it.

"Deal."

I finished my stew and he gave me another bowl. And then another. He fed me until I was warm again. Until I was so full I was afraid I might burst. He gave me a place to sleep with a lock on the door and a set of clean clothes that were way too big.

And the next day, he gave me a job.

CONNOR

Fifty-eight. *Fifty-nine. Sixty. Sixty-one.*

I counted out the pushups in my head. It was the only thing that could clear my mind, other than a fifth of bourbon. And since I was on duty, pushing my body to the limit was the only option I had.

I ignored the heavy, sore feeling in my muscles. I ignored the buzzing of the fluorescent lights overhead. I ignored the steady stream of guys coming and going from the locker room.

Most of all, I ignored the sting of my sweat as it slinked past the still tender bullet wound in my side. The one that had taken a harmless chunk out of me but hit someone else.

Not just hit. Destroyed. Tore through flesh and bone.

The bullet that had ended my partner's life.

I groaned and stood up as I finished the set. After five sets of a hundred pushups, I was sweaty enough to warrant a shower. Maybe it would wake me up too.

It had been a long fucking day already and I wasn't going home any time soon.

Not that there was anything to go home to.

Anything or anyone.

We were working round the clock to close this one out, and it still felt like we were treading water. It was a tough case that had been going on for years. A local gang was dealing guns and drugs. The body count was high.

Until they'd killed one of our own.

Gang crime was nothing new but since my partner had been killed in the line of duty, it was personal for every federal agent on the East Coast.

But mostly for me. I was consumed by the case. Consumed with finding justice.

But what I really wanted to know was *why not me?*

Danny was gone. I still couldn't fucking believe it. He'd been more than my partner. He'd been my best friend.

It almost seemed disrespectful to think about it now, but Danny had been the consummate joker. He hadn't been the best at his job, but man, the guy made me laugh.

I hadn't laughed once in the six months since he got hit.

We'd been partnered together for years. Where I was dark, he was light. Where he had off-the-wall ideas, I did everything by the numbers. Where he had a high tolerance for paperwork, I had a photographic memory and an uncanny sense for catching killers and scum of every kind.

Where he was charming, I scared the living hell out of people.

They called me the shark because I always smelled blood in the water. And I was getting that feeling tonight. It had me on edge.

That and the nine cups of coffee I'd drank today so far. It was after five and I was still jangling. Didn't matter though. It seemed like I slept only in short spurts these days.

Some of the guys said that was what made me such a cranky bastard. They were too smart to say what we all knew was true. They all thought I was a mean sonofabitch because I was missing Danny.

But I could have told them they were wrong.

I was just born that way.

CASSANDRA

"Another round of shots, Saph."

"You got it."

I didn't smile at Jimmy. He knew I hated it when he called me Saph. It was short for Saphire, on account of my eyes. Some of the old timers called me that, but only when Mason wasn't around.

If anyone so much as looked at me, he had a fit.

Even though he wasn't active, he was still an Untouchable. And no one fucked with the Untouchables.

My guardian angel, the guy who had pulled me out of the rain and off the streets all those years ago, was an outlaw biker. Or he had been in his younger, wilder days.

He still looked pretty wild with his tattoos and the giant Hog he rode to and from the joint. The ride I'd taken with him for years, until I'd saved enough for an old car of my own. The rust bucket, as Mason called it. He'd taken it apart and put it back together so that it ran like a dream.

A dangerously fast dream.

Mason James was the kindest man I'd ever met in my life. I'd been right to trust my instincts all those years ago.

Not that I'd had much of a choice.

Mason owned the bar that all the bikers came to. It was definitely badass central around here. The place smelled like leather and smoke and axel grease.

It smelled like home.

For the past three years I'd worked here. I'd run away from my fifth foster home. Like all the rest it had been a little too cold and a lot too dirty. And the woman who 'kept' it was constantly drunk, with a steady stream of on again off again boyfriends.

A few of which had started to pay me a little *too* much attention.

When one of them cornered me in the kitchen late one night, I'd known it was time to go. I'd kicked the guy where it counted and ran, stopping in my room to grab my few belongings. He'd stood in the hallway, jiggling my doorknob over and over. But the fucker didn't know that I'd perfected my escape plan.

I had fixed the lock weeks before.

And I'd already climbed out the window and down the drain pipe. Twice. I'd hit the ground running and never looked back.

So, here I was. And I could not be happier. Well, I could be happier, technically speaking. But I wasn't too worried.

I knew I was lucky to be alive, and in one piece. I had big plans for the future. I'd passed my GED, but I wanted more. Community college for starters. My own place nearby. And maybe, someday, I could actually have a boyfriend.

If Mason didn't scare the shit out of him first.

I was pretty sure he'd threatened to slowly skin the last guy who'd shown an interest alive. Then he'd mentioned cutting off a few body parts. And all the guy had done was ask for my number.

Yeah, Mason watched a lot of Game of Thrones.

So far, I hadn't been interested enough to argue with him. But I would, if I wanted to. I was over 18 now. I could date.

Technically, I *should* be dating. But Mason was right about one thing.

I probably shouldn't date anyone who I met in the bar.

Sure, regular people came in here sometimes. But they were tourists. And that was mostly for lunch.

Most of the time, it was ninety percent bikers. Some in gangs, some independent. Most of them were in or associated with Mason's old gang, the

Untouchables. Some were from the Hell Raisers, a gang from one town over.

They were the ones who made me nervous.

I knew most of the Untouchables. For the most part they were everything you would imagine when you thought of outlaw bikers. Mean, violent, and loud. They were loyal to a fault though, and they looked after me like one of their own.

But it was the Hell Raisers who were downright scary.

And after the stuff I'd seen, I didn't scare all that easy.

The worst part wasn't that they didn't seem to have a sense of loyalty to anything or anyone. Except for him. Tall, darkly handsome and casually cruel.

The worst part was the he liked me.

Dante, the leader of the Raisers, had taken a definite shine to me. He smiled, left outrageous tips, and kissed my hand. I always wanted to scrub my hand when he did that, and I did, still feeling his lips even when the skin was red and raw. I shivered at the thought of him kissing me anywhere else.

Mason hadn't noticed and I planned to keep it that way. If he did, there would be blood.

And considering how crazy Dante was, I didn't know whose blood it would be.

Mase could hold his own with the best of them. I'd seen him crack skulls when things got rough in the bar. But Dante was younger and unpredictable. I'd seen him put a fork through someone's hand once. He'd had his minions clean up the mess before anyone noticed.

But I'd seen it, and he'd smiled at me, like nothing had happened. Like there wasn't blood pouring off the table like cheap ketchup.

Yeah, Dante was a special kind of crazy, and I didn't want him and Mason tussling over me.

So I just deflected, avoided and stayed well out of arm's reach when the Raisers came in. Dante's eyes might follow me constantly, but he hadn't yet crossed any lines.

At two AM the place was full and I was busy. The moment there was a break in the action I stepped outside to get some of the cool Spring air on my face. I inhaled deeply and froze.

Less than ten feet away, a man was being forced to his knees.

"I warned you."

"Please- no-"

"Too fucking late."

I heard the sound of flesh parting as a knife slid across the man's throat. He clutched at it desperately. There was a horrible gargling sound coming from his mouth as he struggled for air. Then he fell silent. The man holding him let go and he slumped to the ground. Dead. Gone. Really gone.

Fuck. Fuck fuck fuck.

I stepped backwards instinctively and the heel of my boot hit something. A can, I would realize later. At that moment I couldn't think. All I could do was panic. Because the two men in the parking lot turned to stare.

Right at me.

I held perfectly still, praying I was hidden in the shadows.

They spoke softly and one of the men started dragging the body away. The other one walked towards me. Almost like he could see in the dark.

The one who had held the knife.

As he got closer I saw who it was and my fear quadrupled. My heart felt like it was going to pound itself right out of my chest. I whimpered as he stepped closer and I *knew* he had seen me.

The bastard probably *could* see in the dark.

He smiled, a slash of light from inside illuminating his face. He was all harsh angles and scars. And those dark, crazy eyes. He reached out and brushed his knuckles over my face.

I could see blood on his fingers. He still held the knife. I didn't breath. Didn't move.

"Such a pretty little thing..."

I was breathing rapidly, puffing like a tiny little bunny rabbit. He smiled and I felt a chill down my spine. He was going to kill me- he was-

"Run little girl. Run back inside now."

I ran.

CONNOR

The house was dark and quiet. No sounds of cars passing by. No glow of streetlights or rustling of neighbors. I'd picked this place on purpose, for the seclusion.

Long ago, I'd had a vague idea of sharing it with someone, starting a family, fixing it up someday. But it had quickly become my refuge from the world. The idea of renovating had flown out the window, along with the visions of backyard barbecues or a woman sharing my bed.

The cabin was old, some 1950's family idea of a rustic lodge. And I hadn't touched a damn thing. The linoleum, the brick, even some of the original furniture was still here, untouched.

Well, other than some light dusting. I wasn't a damn pig. But it was definitely… retro. Hell, maybe I was retro too.

My mom and sister rolled their eyes every time they came over. Some of the old stuff was cool, even they had to admit that. Some was… not.

Yeah, it could have used a woman's touch.

But the only women who set foot in the place were family, and they had to show up unannounced if they wanted to visit. Lately, it seemed easier to be busy than face the disappointed look in my mother's eye, or the glare in my sister's.

I'd really planned to fix the place up. Paint it at least. Hang shelves and pictures and whatever else a person did when they set down roots.

I'd thought maybe someday I'd make an effort to find a girlfriend, instead of the rare one-night stand after a night of drinking. No phone numbers. No repeat customers.

But I hadn't even had one of those in a good long while. That was years ago, when I was coming up in the agency. Now... well, I spent most of my time working or alone.

For the most part, I liked it that way.

It was easier to just ignore the occasional hormonal urge. It's not like anyone had even caught my eye. Not for years.

Hell, I'd forgotten what a woman felt like.

And now... well, I didn't care about anything but catching my partner's killer. I wouldn't be any good for a woman anyway. I was obsessed. Not to mention ill-tempered.

Ring ring.

I opened one eye a crack. It was after 4 am. Nothing good ever came from a phone call at this hour.

I picked up my phone as it rang again. Just as it abruptly went silent. Great, I missed the call *and* it woke my ass up.

Should have put the fucking thing on silent.

I sat up as I read the texts that had been coming in for twenty minutes. Basically, since the moment I'd finally laid down. I hadn't slept more than a few minutes but I was instantly alert.

There was a body found in the road along Route 57. Out near The Mason Jar. Where most of the suspects in my case went to get hammered and beat the shit out of each other.

Well, fuck me.

I was up and on my feet in a heartbeat. The Mason Jar was owned by a guy who was associated with the Untouchables. One of the gangs we were investigating. Mason kept his nose relatively clean, but as far as I could see it, he was swimming in a pool of filth.

The truth was, I had sort of grudgingly liked the guy on the two occasions we'd met. But all that changed after Danny got shot. I squashed any inkling of kindness or comraderie I felt over Mason's seriously well-curated jukebox or the rare, top-shelf whiskeys he kept in a locked case behind the bar.

The man might like the blues and good booze but he was still a criminal. And he knew the killer of the brother I'd never had. So as far as I was concerned, he was the enemy.

I would never set foot in his joint, except to interrogate the bastard.

But this- this might lead us in the right direction. A turning point to finally pin something on the Hell Raisers. Or any of the local gangs really. They were all culpable.

Anyone who had even so much as breathed near Danny's killer was on my hit list. And I meant to take them all down.

They were all guilty by association.

I splashed water on my face and hopped in the car without even making a pot of coffee. There was a stale cup in the cup holder and I slugged it down, wincing at the bitter taste.

Stale, cold coffee... yeah, I was pretty sure that was my blood type at this point. It was the reason I never took milk with it. Black coffee stayed drinkable a hell of a lot longer.

I should know.

I drove the forty-five minutes in absolute silence. My mind was clear. I liked to go into any crime scene situation completely blank.

Clean.

Open.

I saw the flashing lights. They were less than twenty yards from the parking lot of The Jar. Whoever had done this had either been in a hurry or didn't give a shit about pissing Mason off.

That was the first clue. There was no way this was an Untouchable. Even if Mason wasn't active, they wouldn't shit where they ate.

But someone who didn't like Mason... well, this was a real good way to cause trouble for him.

I imagined he was pretty pissed off right about now. My suspicions were confirmed as I pulled up to the bar and parked.

Mason stood out front, his arms crossed over his massive chest.

I could almost see the steam coming out of his ears. He nodded to me and went back to staring at the crime scene.

That's when I saw it.

At edge of the parking lot, not far from the scene was a smoking bike. It had been torched.

I stared at it, my mind absorbing visual clues, sorting them into facts and feelings.

I had a hunch that the killer, or killers, had toasted the victim's bike, but not to make it look like an accident. This already looked like plain old murder. These guys didn't value life the way ordinary folks did.

But this was unusual. Little was done to hide the crime. The fire wasn't meant to hide evidence.

No. This was an insult to the dead man. Sort of like spitting on someone's grave. I'd actually heard of guys getting buried *with* their wheels.

A biker's ride was an extension of his body. I knew the feeling. I had a ride myself.

So whatever else we knew about the vic, he'd clearly pissed someone off. Not just a little either. He'd pissed them off a lot.

I walked the perimeter, circling inward towards the crime scene. It was dark in the back, but my eyes were sharp. I used a flashlight intermittently, turning it on and off to see what the light revealed, as well as the dark.

I spotted an area that looked like a body might have been dragged and a spreading pool that looked like motor oil, or more likely, blood. I whistled and got forensics to photograph the area and mark it off until samples could be taken.

Only then did I look at the body.

He was on his back, his blank eyes staring up at the sky. His throat had been cut. But that wasn't all that had been done to him.

No, they'd cut his tongue out too. After the fact. You could tell that without forensics, because there should have been more blood.

As it was, he was positively clean looking. I had a feeling all his blood was back in the parking lot. It was not a pleasant way to go, never mind what they'd done to his bike.

All of that took time. Not just five minutes either. Ten or twenty. I started to mentally clock it all out in my head.

Who the hell would stick around a crime scene to mutilate a body and then set fire to the victim's ride? Someone who wasn't afraid of the law, that was for sure.

Someone batshit fucking crazy.

And I had a good fucking idea of who that might be.

I went inside and took a look around. The bar was nearly empty. They must have been closing up when the bike went up in flames. Everyone had taken off after that.

Everyone but the staff.

I saw Mason with his hand resting possessively on a girl's shoulder. She sat at the bar, her arms wrapped around her protectively. I could only see her profile but even that was enough to stop me in my tracks.

All thoughts of murder flew from my head.

The girl was beautiful.

Not just a little bit pretty, or cute, or even sexy. She was fucking gorgeous. With long, wavy, light brown hair, and a delicate profile with a nose that was just the slightest bit turned upwards. Her figure looked slim and athletic, but with curves in all the right places.

She turned to look at me and my breath stopped. My heart seemed to pause, waiting for my mind to catch up with my eyeballs, which felt like they were bugging out of my damn head.

She was a Goddamned angel.

Even in this smokey juke joint, with the dim lights and neon beer signs, I could see her eyes.

They were the brightest, deepest blue I'd seen in my life. And I was a fan of staring at the sky, or I had been when I had less shit to worry about.

This was the blue of *ten thousands* skies.

She blinked and I came back to myself. The girl might have the face of an angel but right now she was part of a crime scene. If she worked here, she most likely knew the killer, or at least served him a bucket of wings.

Which meant under my rules, she was part of the problem. The fact that I had such a strong reaction to her only pissed me off. Why the hell work here with all the criminals when she could be plastered all over billboards and magazine covers?

Because she was one of them. The enemy. The ones who had killed Danny.

Remember that, Conn.

I forced myself to ignore the hot pulse of lust that was throbbing in my belly and crossed the bar. I flashed my badge and pulled out a tiny note pad. Yeah, I was old school in that way too.

"Name."

"They already interviewed me."

"Not you."

They exchanged a glance and Mason stepped in front of her.

"She ain't got nothin' to do with this, DeWitt."

I let myself steal another look at her. Her huge eyes were looking down at the ground. Her juicy bottom lip was caught between Chiclet white teeth. I squinted at Mason and asked again.

"Name."

"It's okay, Mase."

She cleared her throat and Mason sighed heavily, stepping aside. I was once again struck by the girl's absolute physical perfection. And the nervous look in her eyes.

Good.

She should be fucking nervous. I wasn't going to go easy on her because she was stunningly beautiful. Or young. Or scared.

I realized belatedly that the girl looked more than scared. She was frightened out of her mind. That made me want to tell her that everything would be okay. That I would take care of everything for her.

I frowned, disquieted by the swirl of protective and animalistic urges that she was causing. Unwanted urges, dammit.

"Casey. Casey Jones."

Her voice was soft and sweet, stirring something even warmer inside me. But something felt off. It felt like a lie. Maybe it wasn't her real name. I leaned against the bar, musing over how young she looked.

Too young for me.

The thought caught me off guard. Now where the hell had that come from? Completely out of left field. Not only was it true, but I certainly didn't date criminal trash.

I glanced at Mason who was frowning at me, a worried look on his face. He cared about the girl, that much was obvious. I had a moment of pure animal jealousy, wondering if he was screwing her.

Why I cared, I had no fucking idea.

But I did. I cared a lot.

I gave Mason a hard look.

"Is she your wife?"

"No."

"Girlfriend?"

He shook his head and some of the tension left my body. I felt a strange relief that made no sense at all. I should not give a damn one way or the other.

But I was almost friendly as I nodded to Mason.

"Then you have to step away, Mason. Sorry."

"I'm responsible for her, dammit!"

Well, that was unexpected. Maybe she was his kid. I looked at her again. Hmm, no. He wasn't *that* much older.

Unless he had a kid at fourteen.

"Is she your child? Relation?"

He shook his head. I glanced at the girl, my eyes skimming over her graceful curves. She really was perfect. She looked like one of those girls in those sexy bra commercials.

Lush and young and desirable.

And way too clean and innocent to be in a place like this. But she wasn't innocent. At the very least, she was a prime witness.

"Is she underage?"

"I'm old enough to work here. I don't serve drinks."

I felt something hitch in my stomach at that. Damn, she *was* young. Not even twenty-one.

I definitely shouldn't be having the sort of thoughts I was having. Thoughts about touching her. Kissing her. Taking her to my bed and tangling up the sheets.

No. I should not be thinking any of that, dammit. And not just because she was involved in a crime.

Not just because she was so young either.

She was one of *them*. The people who had killed my partner.

I'd just met the girl. Never before in my life had I taken one look at a female and thought- I would like to hold her all night.

Not just all night either. I had a crazy feeling I'd like to hold her a lot longer than that.

Well, fuck.

CASSANDRA

The guy wasn't a regular cop. Mason had whispered 'FBI' to me as soon as he'd walked in the door.

I'd barely even registered his words.

I was too busy staring at the best-looking man I'd ever seen in my life. With his impossibly pretty, blue green eyes, muscular build and chiseled face, he was the quintessential good guy.

He looked like the hero in one of those old Westerns Mason loved to watch on Sundays. He'd cook up a huge batch of chili or stew or barbecue and we'd settle in on the couch to watch old movies.

Mason called those Sunday sessions his church. And I sort of got why. Those Sunday afternoon movie fests had been one of the most reliable things in my entire life.

Well, *after.*

I used to think of my life as two lives- now three. 'Before' my parents died I'd been a happy suburban kid. Then a car accident had claimed them both.

In one split-second they were gone.

The people from child protective services had come and taken me from the neighbor who had taken me in those first few days. We didn't have any other family. So just like that, I was a ward of the state.

Then there was 'after.'

Foster homes. State housing. Bad food and cold nights.

And then there was 'Mason.'

I had a feeling I was going to start thinking of my life as four completely different lives after tonight. The night I'd seen something I shouldn't have. The night I became a problem for someone like Dante to solve.

No one knew I'd seen a thing. Not even Mason.

I just prayed that my silence would be enough.

Now, this ridiculously gorgeous man was looking at me like I was scum. I bristled. He might be on the right side of the law but I hadn't done anything wrong.

Well, not yet. But I was about to.

The moment I told him I hadn't seen a thing, I was an accessory. At least I thought so anyway. I knew it was wrong to withhold information about any crime, let alone a murder.

But I had no choice. For my sake, but especially for Mason's.

Because I knew Dante wouldn't be satisfied with my death if I squealed. He would want to make sure I hadn't told anyone else either.

He'd come after Mason too.

The giant FBI agent was staring at me. He must have asked a question but I'd blanked out on it. He raised his eyebrows and asked me again.

"Were you on duty when the crime was committed?"

I opened my mouth and prepared to lie.

CONNOR

"I don't know when the crime was committed. But I've been on since six."

Lie.

I felt it in my gut. And it bothered me.

People lied to federal agents all the time. It was part of the deal. But for some reason, this felt worse.

Maybe because I knew without a doubt that this girl was innocent. She might be in this world, but she was not *of* it. At least that's what my gut was telling me.

I was well aware that it might have something to do with the way my dick was feeling at the moment.

Hard. And getting harder.

I cleared my throat, glad I was wearing a suit jacket. I was in jeans too thankfully, which were thick enough to hold my stiff cock in place.

Jesus Con, get a grip.

Fucking typical. After years of ignoring the female species, I find a girl that catches my attention and she's off limits. More than off limits, this little girl was *forbidden.*

By law.

Still, I could hear Danny whispering in my ear. *She's a real peach Conn... why don't you pluck her?*

"So you didn't see anything?"

She shook her head, looking away. I narrowed my eyes. She was a terrible liar. For some reason, I liked that about her.

Even if it was making my job harder than it had to be.

Mason was watching from across the room, pacing like a caged tiger. I jerked my head and he came over.

"I'm taking her in."

"Don't do this DeWitt. You're putting a target on her back."

"I'm only telling you as a courtesy."

Mason's jaw twitched. I knew what he was saying. But I didn't agree. Anyone who had been in the bar that night might be a witness. She was here, and she wasn't drunk like most of the clientele.

Didn't matter that his panties were in a bunch. Didn't matter how adorable the girl was or that she made my dick twitch. I needed to show the waitress pictures.

"Take me too."

I shook my head slowly. "No." I knew that he would never snitch. Mason was the world's least effective witness against another biker. I also knew he spent most of the night alone in his office. And I could tell the girl knew more than she was letting on.

Plus, the other agents had already interviewed Mason. The girl was fresh meat. He must have kept her hidden in the back. I'd walked in at just the right moment.

I stared at her. She looked so small and delicate. But she was definitely a woman. Curvy and soft and sweet.

She lifted her chin and stared right back. Not a coward then. That was good.

Because it was going to be a long fucking night.

"Come on."

I put my hand on her shoulder as we left the bar. It was true that if people saw her with me they might think she was talking. But I thought it was safe enough. No one was around at this hour unless they were hiding in the damn bushes. Besides, it couldn't be helped.

I ignored the little thrill of anticipation I felt as we walked to the car. I was going to be spending some quality time getting to know little Miss Casey Jones.

Starting with the ride back to headquarters.

I opened the passenger side door and watched as she slid in. I stifled a smirk as she buckled up. She crossed her legs at the ankles and stared straight ahead.

She seemed like a good girl, with her hair neatly braided over one shoulder and her neatly manicured nails.

It made me want to mess up her hair. Feel her nails scratch my back. Ruffle those perfect feathers of hers.

In the filthiest way possible.

But I also wanted to find out how she ended up working at The Jar. And why Mason said he was responsible for her.

And I had almost an hour to find out.

CASSANDRA

"Ⓗow do you know Mason?"

I was silent, staring out the window. Honestly, I felt like I was in shock. I guess that's what happened when you saw someone get slaughtered in front of you like a pig.

"Casey."

There was such a firm authority in his voice. It made me want to answer him, at the same time it made me want to defy him. I'd been such a well-behaved child. The first to raise her hand, the last to talk in class.

But after I got shuffled into the foster care system, well, I had stopped trusting authority figures.

Living with an outlaw biker had only deepened that sense of distrust.

"He's my uncle."

"He is?"

I shrugged.

"Kind of. He's a distant relation. He took me in."

I had to tell him something. And that was as close to the truth as I could get without saying *'I was a teenage runaway and he saved me from a life on the streets.'*

Of course, in my case I hadn't been on the streets all that long. A week at most, but when I thought back on those days, it felt like much longer. I was more than lucky. It was a miracle I hadn't wound up in a ditch, or worse, getting trafficked like so many teenage runaways did.

If this guy thought I was going to put Mason in danger after saving me from all that, well he had another thing coming.

"He's not bad. For a biker."

I shot him a look. That was an odd thing to say. He was playing good cop, bad cop with me. He had to be.

But he looked sincere.

"What's your name?"

I don't know why I asked, or why I cared. I was supposed to be a brick wall. Silent. Unless I wanted to get myself and the only person I cared about left on Earth killed.

Worse than killed. Gutted. Slaughtered.

I shivered, thinking of the guy in the parking lot. Hearing him beg.

"DeWitt." He cleared his throat. "Connor DeWitt."

I said nothing, sinking lower into the seat. I was so tired but there was no way I could sleep. I could feel the adrenalin pumping through my body. Every inch of me, every nerve was awake.

I closed my eyes and immediately saw Dante bending over the begging man. I saw him come close, seeing me in the darkness. I felt him stroke my cheek.

I'd spent twenty minutes in the bathroom washing my face after that. But I could still feel his touch.

I shivered again, wrapping my arms around my shoulders.

"Are you cold?"

He turned the heat up without waiting for my answer. Then he did something so unexpected it took me completely by surprise.

Federal Agent Connor Dewitt draped his expensive looking jacket over me like a blanket.

CONNOR

I sipped my coffee, staring through the one way mirror.

Casey Jones was sitting behind a heavy steel table, bolted to the floor. With her long, graceful neck and dewy skin, she looked utterly out of place in such a cold, industrial setting.

She looked like she should be running through a Goddamn field of flowers. Or riding a horse in one of those soap commercials. Or... I don't know, sitting by a fire surrounded by kittens.

With a man's arms around her.

I realized that the man in my mind's eye was way too familiar. I'd pictured myself holding her. Where the hell was that coming from? She was one of them. Don't be fooled by those big, beautiful eyes.

Focus Dewitt.

I opened the door.

"I got you a coffee."

She looked up at me, her face frightened. Again I thought, she does not belong here. But I was the one who had brought her in.

"Let's start at the beginning. You came in for your shift at six pm."

She nodded and tucked her hair behind her ear. The gesture was so childlike, I almost flinched. She really was barely old enough to be here without a parent.

But she didn't have parents. She had Mason.

"Yes."

"And during the course of the evening, did you notice anything strange. Any altercations?"

She shook her head, pulling her knees up and wrapping her arms around them. Again, I felt a flush of guilt. She looked like a little girl, playing dress up.

"Are you cold?"

She'd insisted on giving me back my jacket but I was more than happy to hand it back to her. It had smelled so good when I put it on in the parking lot. I had to stop myself from sniffing it.

Like honeysuckle and sunshine.

I grimaced, glad no one could hear my thoughts. I sounded ridiculous. Like some love-struck hero in a romance novel.

"I'm fine."

She didn't look fine. She looked tired and scared and cold. Probably hungry too.

"When is the last time you ate?"

She took a sip of her coffee and shook her head again.

"I'm okay."

"When?"

She almost rolled her eyes at me and I had a moment of sympathy for Mason. He'd brought this girl up. And I had a feeling that she could give as good as she got. Maybe it was the stubborn little chin, but I could tell Casey Jones had backbone.

I grinned at the thought of the burly biker trying to tell the girl she was grounded.

"Before my shift. It got busy and I just- forgot."

Well, fuck. No wonder she looked woozy. I decided to get her something to eat as soon as we got through the interview. Before I showed her the mugshots.

Considering how uncommunicative she was being, I had a feeling that wasn't going to be productive. But I was doing this by the book with zero deviation.

I didn't want anyone saying I was going easy on her because I wanted to toss her over my shoulder and run off with her. Even if it was true.

She was so small, I could probably lift her with one arm.

I leaned back and stared at her.

"Not one thing. No fights. In a biker bar?"

43

She shrugged.

"Not that I noticed."

Well, this was going nowhere.

"So when did you find out about the body?"

"When I heard the sirens."

I frowned. It was possible that she hadn't seen anything. But highly unlikely. For her sake I almost wished it was true.

For a second, I found myself wondering what she would think of me if we had met under other circumstances. If a cute little thing like her would consider a stiff like me.

Especially considering the crowd she ran with.

But the truth was, I would never let myself get close enough to find out. I hated them too much. All of them.

Even her.

"Did you wait on the victim?"

"I still don't know who the victim is."

I slid a picture across the table. It had been easy to find. Forensics had taken the guy's fingerprints before they even carted the body off.

And the vic had a rap sheet a mile long.

"Dustin Scott. He's a pretty scummy character." I smiled grimly, raising my eyebrows. "Or, he *was*."

She chewed her lip and I wondered again how she'd ended up in this mess. She could do a hell of a lot better than waiting tables in a dive bar, that was for sure.

"He was at the bar I think. Did he have a beard?"

I shook my head. I had a feeling she was deflecting. But that didn't mean anything. She could just be shaken up because there'd been a damn murder.

Or because she was in an interrogation room. They weren't exactly designed to be comfortable.

But that wasn't what my gut was telling me.

My gut was telling me that she knew something. Maybe, just maybe, she knew *everything*.

She was the only person who had a reason to be in the back, near where I'd found the drag marks and blood. There wasn't another waitress on that night, and the bartender had sworn up and down he never left the bar except to whiz.

Fuck it, I might as well get on with it.

"Do you know this man?"

I pushed the photo of Dante across the table. I saw her stiffen up. She barely glanced at it. She acted like it was a snake that might bite her.

Well, that answered that. She knew him alright. I felt a weird heavy feeling settle in my gut. It felt like dread.

Her slender shoulders lifted in an imperceptible shrug.

"He comes in sometimes."

"Do you know who he is?"

She looked at me and I saw it. She *did* know. I saw how lost and scared she was. And how tough. But also how good.

And dammit it if I didn't want to take care of her.

"He's a biker."

I leaned back in my seat and smiled at her. I couldn't help it. I'd wanted to smile since the moment I set eyes on her.

"He's the president of the Hell Raisers."

She chewed her lip again and I stared, the gesture sending a hot shot of lust right to my groin. Something about that pouty lower lip... I could do things with that mouth.

Dark and dirty things.

I cleared my throat.

"Let me get you something to eat. I'll be right back."

She frowned at me.

"I told you everything."

"We still need to go over a few more things. You eat, I ask. And then I'll take you home."

CASSANDRA

"Do you usually go without eating for so long?"

I was chewing on the surprisingly good turkey sandwich the agent had brought me. He was being oddly nice to me. The guy seemed decent, for the law.

Being a runaway had taught me not to trust the law.

Living with Mason had just reinforced that over the years.

"No. It was busy tonight."

Shit. Say nothing Cass! Say nothing!

But that wasn't really much of a clue. Still, the less I said the better. I needed to be smart if I wanted to keep Mason alive.

Never mind myself.

I knew with a heavy certainty that I only had a slim chance to escape Dante's wrath. The fact that he'd let me walk out of that parking lot at all was the only reason I wasn't running for the damn border.

That and the guy sitting across from me.

He watched me eat, playing with a pen with one hand. I caught myself staring at his hand. It was tanned and thick, but still graceful. It looked... strong. Like he worked outdoors with his hands.

He'd taken his jacket off, trying to get me to wear it again. It felt too intimate to take it so I'd shook him off, even though I *was* cold.

Without the jacket I could see just how fit the agent was. Not just fit, either. He was buff. His muscles had muscles. But he didn't look like a meathead.

He was just... perfect.

I squinted my nose and popped another potato chip in my mouth. *Ugh, stop mooning over the enemy, Cass!* He didn't rush me to finish my meal. Just stared at me with those deep blue green eyes.

For a minute, I wondered if this was part of the interrogation. Maybe he was trying to unsettle me with his good manners. I'd have to ask Mason later. Conner was being so nice.

Too nice.

Maybe all of this would end up in a report later. In a permanent file. Subject snarfed potato chips like a little piggy. Subject has questionable footwear. Subject has body odor.

I took a little sniff under my shirt, suddenly afraid that I did smell.

Maybe that's why he kept giving me his jacket.

I pushed the tray away abruptly. I had eaten almost every damn bite. Even the little carton of chocolate milk.

Jeez, did the guy think I was five years old or something?

I sat up straighter, suddenly annoyed at being treated like a kid. The truth was though, I did love my chocolate milk.

"So. How long have you worked at The Jar?"

I stared at him, trying to think of a reasonable lie. Then I gave up. If it was illegal to have me working there at sixteen, so be it.

"When I was fifteen."

He raised his eyebrows.

"Mason put you to work, huh?"

"I wanted to work. I don't like charity."

"Seems like a rough spot for a teenage girl."

I raised my chin and stared at him.

"I've seen worse."

We held each other's eyes. Something flickered in his richly colored gaze. It seemed like he almost felt sorry for me. Then he smiled.

"That's too bad."

I blinked. He meant it. My gut was screaming at me that this guy was the real deal. He wasn't just playing good cop. Why did that make me feel so safe?

I rubbed my eyes, suddenly tired. The adrenaline from earlier must be wearing off. I yawned and he smiled at me again.

He stood and jerked his head towards the door.

"Come on, I'll drive you home."

CONNOR

The truth was, I should have kept her a few more hours. I had more pictures to show her. And I wanted to break her, get to the bottom of this.

My partner's life demanded it. Or the life he should have had. Would have had, if not for the local scum.

So why the hell didn't you, Conn?

I was getting soft. That must be it. A pretty girl, a pair of big eyes with long legs and I was toast.

Soggy toast that had been slathered in warm butter.

Soft. Weak. But at the moment, I didn't much care.

I was too busy enjoying her company in the quiet intimacy of the car. It was like a cocoon, separate from reality. I glanced over and resisted the urge to stretch out a hand, to let my finger drag over her skin.

I could probably have gotten away with it. Just one touch to see if her skin was as impossibly soft as it looked. Just her cheek.

No one would ever know. Not even her.

The delicate looking girl beside me had fallen asleep.

She looked even younger in her sleep, and my protective instincts were in overdrive. I didn't just want to take her home safely tonight. I didn't even just want to kiss her, and everything that came after.

I wanted to protect her.

To keep her safe.

And considering the world I'd plucked her out of, that was far from easy.

But that wasn't the strangest part. I shook my head, keeping my eyes on the road. The strangest part was how awake I felt. How alive.

It was the first time I'd thought about anything but revenge in... well, almost a year.

I cleared my throat and she stirred, stretching those insanely nice legs of hers and blinking up at me like a sleepy little owl.

A hot and sexy owl. But still somehow freaking sweet and adorable at the same time.

Harmless. She looked utterly harmless. Except to my peace of mind. And my cock.

In that regard, she was incredibly dangerous.

"You said Lewiston. I need a street address."

She blinked again and the wall went up. I saw it happen. And I hated it.

Damn, I'd really preferred the soft and sleepy little kitten.

"47 Charles."

I gave her a sharp glance. I knew that address. I'd had it under casual surveillance in the past, before I realized Mason was straight.

Or mostly straight, for a biker.

"You live with Mason?"

"Yeah."

"You said you were his... niece?"

She gave me a look. She knew what I was asking. I suddenly had the unpleasant image of her wrapped up in the burly bikers arms, his big hands all over her-

"He's not a perv. He's looked after me since I was fifteen."

Something clicked. Fifteen...

"When you started at The Jar."

It wasn't a question. She looked away, slinking down into the seat the way only a teenage girl could. Only she wasn't a teenager anymore. Or, she wouldn't be much longer.

She was legal.

Christ Conn, get your mind out of the gutter!

"You're a stray aren't you?"

She glared at me. I could tell she wanted to tell me to fuck off. I grinned suddenly, overjoyed that

Mason wasn't her man. That didn't make a damn bit of sense either.

It's not like I could date her anyway for God's sake.

It was crazy to even think about it. It could never happen. *Never.* Not for a million reasons.

1. She was too damn young.
2. She was too damn pretty.
3. She was part of the seedy underbelly that I meant to gauge out and expose.
4. She was a Goddamn WITNESS.
5. Danny. She could be the key to avenging Danny's death.

I realized I was gripping the wheel so hard my hands were turning white. I exhaled deeply and rolled the window down, letting a shot of cold air hit my face. I glanced at her and rolled it back up again.

It might be stupid, but I loved seeing her wear my jacket.

I pulled over in front of Mason's house and put the car in park. I turned to her, making an effort to remember this was not a date.

Because I had the unmistakable urge to kiss her.

Get it together, Conn!

"We're here."

She pulled off the jacket and I got hit with that wave again. The sweet, feminine smell of her. Her hair got caught in the seatbelt and I had to clench my fist to keep from pulling it free for her.

After a second I gave in, my hands brushing the back of her neck as I tugged the silky strands loose. I inhaled sharply. My fingers felt like they'd been electrified by the feel of her skin. But not in a bad way.

In a fucking miraculous way.

I knew without a doubt that I was going to be hard for hours. Just from that. I stifled a groan and leaned away from her. It was the hardest damn thing I'd ever done in my life, too.

She gave me a small nod. She was such a serious little thing. I stared at her, my body urging me to make a move. I smiled reassuringly. Or tried to. I'm sure it looked like a grimace.

"Thanks, for the ride I guess."

"Don't worry. We'll be seeing each other soon."

I watched her as she walked down the path and disappeared around the side of the house. I sat there for a little while, lost in thought. The sun was coming up, so I put on my shades and drove away.

CASSANDRA

W*e'll be seeing each other soon.*

His words echoed in my head as I walked up the walkway to the side door. It swung open and I was engulfed in a bear hug of epic proportions.

"Case- Jesus girl, I have been worried sick."

I looked at him. Mason was pale. He did look worried. I grimaced.

"Sorry, Mace. I was kind of busy."

"You never heard of a damned text message?"

I shrugged. He was right. I'd been totally distracted by the big detective. Is that what he was? Or was he an agent?

Either way, I'd been distracted by the big guy in the suit.

I shivered, wrapping my arms around my chest. It had gotten really cold. Mornings often were this close to the water.

Mason cursed and sat me down at the kitchen table. He plopped a bowl of oatmeal down in front of me and started cutting slices of banana into it.

"Eat."

He left and came back with a blanket. He wrapped it around my shoulders.

"We can talk later. Unless you want to tell me something now?"

He was staring at me, the look in his eyes intense. No one was as loyal as Mason. And he cared about me. He was literally my only 'person.'

Alive, anyway.

I shrugged. I had the sudden urge to tell him everything. To unburden myself. But that would only put his life in danger.

So I held my tongue.

"I didn't have much to tell them."

"Were they mean to you? I'll kill DeWitt if he-"

I shook my head vehemently.

"Connor? He was... nice."

Mason stared at me, his mouth slightly open.

"DeWitt? Nice?"

"Yeah. He brought me coffee and a sandwich and stuff. He even loaned me his jacket so I wouldn't be cold."

Mason sat back in his chair, a strange look on his face. Then, unexpectedly, he started laughing.

Not just laughing. Guffawing.

I'm not sure I'd ever heard him laugh that hard in all the years I'd known him. He reached down and scratched Besos behind the ear as the scruffy dog looked back and forth between us, whining. I knew he wanted to lick my bowl clean.

Besos was a weird dog. He really loved oatmeal. Probably because he'd lived on the streets as a stray for so long. He'd learned to survive. He'd take whatever he could get.

I knew the feeling.

"What?"

"Nothing, Casey. He's just the biggest hard-ass I've ever met. The man doesn't 'do' nice."

"He doesn't? That's weird."

"I think Connor might have a little crush."

I spooned more oatmeal into my mouth. The food was so good and so warm, I could have eaten a bathtub full. It was kind of like that first night. I'd sat right here, soaking wet and gorging myself on Mason's homemade stew. Even with the sandwich earlier, I was starving.

Facing down Dante and the FBI in one night could do that to a girl.

Maybe that's why it took a few seconds for Mason's word to register.

"Huh?"

"Connor. He doesn't do nice. He must have it bad if he was that friendly."

I rolled my eyes. Mason had been warning me for years that I was going to get male attention. More than I'd want most likely. He'd told me not to trust men. He'd taught me how to defend myself too.

So far, it hadn't been an issue.

Mason kind of made sure of it.

"I doubt it. He was just doing his job."

"Oh trust me, he thought you were a peach. Too bad for Connor, he's never gonna get a taste."

He reached forward and gently tugged on my nose. I wrinkled it up and he laughed again.

"Come on, kid. You better take a hot shower and get into bed."

Mason had a way of being parental without rubbing me the wrong way. He wasn't bossy, so much as the voice of mature reason. I nodded and headed to the shower, my mind pleasantly numb.

But when I slid under the covers ten minutes later I couldn't get the idea out of my head. I twirled my wet hair around a finger and snuggled lower into the soft sheets.

Mason thought the suit had a crush on me.

But when I closed my eyes, all I could see was blood.

CONNOR

"**Y**ou should get some sleep."

I rubbed my eyes and shrugged. Sheila had a point. I'd come in after dropping off the girl and started right in on my report.

And digging. Lots of digging.

Not all of it pertaining to the murdered biker either.

There was a certain little waitress who was lodged in my brain, keeping me going. I wanted to get to the bottom of who, and what, she really was.

But Sheil was right. I needed to stay sharp. I gave her a smile.

"Yes, Ma."

She rolled her eyes and made a rude hand gesture. *There she was.* Sheila McCafferty was one hell of an agent. She'd been around the block, though she wasn't quite an old-timer.

Still, she'd been around way before me.

From the get-go she'd been rude and compassionate at the same time. Like a tired woman that can't help but love her redheaded stepchildren, no matter how many times they tracked mud through the kitchen.

She was as likely to make you homemade soup for lunch as to slap you upside the head for doing something stupid. And she was more likely to zing you if she liked you. I knew, because I'd always been one of her favorites.

She'd school the younger agents on the ins and outs of proper protocol, let you know which shortcuts were okay and which were not, and embarrass the hell out of you by being faster and stronger than most of the new recruits.

Then she'd bring in homemade muffins the next day. Good ones too.

Yep, Sheila was a certified badass at fifty.

Like everyone else, I loved her to bits.

She reminded me of my mom's older sister, who we'd lost a few years back. My mom had always been a little scared of her sister Maggie, who had no children of her own. She was tough and authoritative. But she'd been the glue that held the family together.

The holidays just weren't the same without her.

But I had a second family. My fellow agents were like blood relations to me. And Sheil was without a doubt the one that held us all together, through the hard times especially. I knew I wouldn't have made it through this last year without her.

61

I wondered for a second what Sheil would think of my weird fixation on the gorgeous little waitress from The Jar. She'd probably smack the back of my head and tell me to snap out of it. And she'd be right.

Not that it would work. It would take more than a head slap to cure me. It had been less than twenty-four hours, and I hadn't stopped thinking about the girl since I'd met her.

I'd already run a background check and come up with nothing. Maybe it didn't matter for the case, but I had a funny hunch that there was something there to find. And I wanted to know all her secrets before I interviewed her again.

Oh yeah, I wanted to learn all about pretty little Casey Jones.

I rubbed my eyes and shut down the laptop, deciding to bring it home with me. I'd get a few hours of shut eye and then start up again.

Maybe I'd even make a house call. Run some surveillance.

Solve the mystery of Mason and his barely legal little house mate.

I grimaced at the word 'mate,' my thoughts immediately filling with vivid images of her ripe little body. And not just her body.

I was in those visions too.

Without even trying I could conjure up images of us together. Kissing. Rolling around together. Screwing like rabbits.

Jesus Conn, take a cold shower why don't you?

Danny's voice was in my head again. As usual, he called me on my shit. Even dead, he was a pain in my ass. But I knew he was right. I did the next best thing, splashing cold water on my face and head before I took to the road.

I drove home carefully, taking side roads. I was bone weary but I knew how to stay alert. It was part of the job. But I knew better than most that a car was a weapon and had to be treated with the same respect as a loaded firearm.

I left the windows open and left the radio off.

I was a longtime member of the insomnia club, so I knew the drill. But I had a feeling I was going to have no problem at all getting some sleep, middle of the day or not.

At home I didn't bother to undress or shower. I just laid down and that was it. I was out.

I cracked my eyes open with a moan, blinking as I looked around the darkening room. It was already evening from the looks of it. My thoughts went immediately to her.

Yes, I was awake just in time for me to pay a little visit.

I smiled grimly at the thought. I was going to find out who killed that biker. And if Casey Jones was the key to that, so be it.

It had nothing to do with how appealing she was. Not a damn thing.

I'd protect her the way I would protect any other witness. No more, and no less.

I'd passed out with one foot on the floor. When was the last time I had slept that deeply? Years maybe. I stretched and kicked my shoes off.

Damn, I had slept like a rock.

A hot shower and two cups of coffee set me right. I checked my email, reviewing some of the forensic reports that were starting to come in.

No fingerprints on the body, but plenty of fibers. No DNA as of yet. Not surprisingly, the corpse had a blood alcohol level that would have sunk an elephant.

I shook my head. What a waste. Well, at least he hadn't felt what they did to him after. I didn't give a shit about the criminal element, but I didn't think anyone deserved to die like that.

Cut up like a piece of meat.

It wasn't just gruesome and violent. It was despicable. And something about it felt even more unhinged that the average murder scene.

Murder of any kind was pretty unhinged. I'd taken life in the line of duty. But never lightly. And it weighed heavily on me every time.

But this had been done casually. It was blatant. And it almost seemed like... well, it seemed like the killer, or killers, had been having *fun*.

There was nothing pointing to a crime motivated by greed or territory wars. The Untouchables weren't at war with anyone. And the business with the burnt bike and the mutilation- There was definitely something psychotic about the whole thing.

I drove towards Charles Street, my fingers tapping the steering wheel. Without even thinking, I turned on my favorite classic rock station after I got off the highway. I couldn't remember the last time I had done that.

There was a pep in my step as I headed up the walkway to Mason's house. I knew there was a good chance the girl wasn't even home. Or that they both were, and he'd make my job more difficult.

But the lights were on, and I was feeling lucky.

I put one hand on my gun and pressed the doorbell.

Ding dong.

CASSANDRA

I was curled up on the couch in my pajamas, flipping through reality shows when I heard it. Footsteps outside. But they didn't sound Mason.

No, definitely not biker boots.

I exhaled, realizing my heart had been pounding. I felt like a tiny little bunny, praying there wasn't a wolf outside the briar patch. Yeah, I was pretty much in fight or flight mode.

And I didn't much like it.

The doorbell rang. I sort of doubted Dante would ring the doorbell. I swallowed and padded over to the door in my fuzzy slippers.

I peeked out the window with the faded curtain and froze. It was him. The suit was here.

The federal freaking agent was standing outside the door.

The really hot one.

I closed my eyes and prayed for strength. Then I did the only thing I could do. I opened the door.

"It's a little early for bunnies, isn't it?"

Bunnies? How did he know what I had just been thinking? I glanced down at my feet.

Oh, right. My slippers. Wake up, Cass.

Fantastic, Mr. Genetically Perfect was seeing me in my PJ's. Not sexy ones either. I was in a cami with an open hooded sweatshirt and flannel polka dot pajama pants. Very dignified.

Not.

"Mase gave me the night off."

He quirked a smile at me and I froze. He looked almost boyish when he smiled. It was disarming. It made me forget who he was and why he was here.

To get me murdered.

Basically this guy, who was reasonably nice and undeniably gorgeous, was going to get me killed.

And Mason. Don't forget about Mason.

"That was nice of him."

I stood there, still staring at the agent. He wasn't in his suit tonight. He was in jeans and a casual button down. But he was still on duty.

Don't forget that. Do not. Forget.

Even if that smile had transformed him completely.

"Um, do you want to sit down?"

He nodded and I stepped back to let him inside.

I got an unexpected whiff of him as he walked past me. He smelled so good. Like the woods where we'd gone camping a few summers ago. Pine and fresh air and something… warm.

He waited for me to lock the door. As big as he was, he managed to fill the small kitchen. I swallowed and led him into the living room.

He watched me like a hawk as I hastened to turn off the TV, embarrassed that the housewives of wherever was on.

He must think I'm an idiot. I *am* an idiot. Why else would I care what he thinks?

You want him to think you are dumb, Cass. Dumb enough not to notice someone getting killed in a parking lot right in front of your eyes.

I folded the blanket I'd been rolled up in and offered him a seat. I sat on the opposite end of the couch from him. For a minute we just sat there.

It felt so weird, like we weren't sure what to say to each other.

I caught Connor staring at me and looked away. Maybe Mason was right... my cheeks got red.

Don't be stupid Cass. He's just here to do his job. It's not a date.

Even if it sort of felt like one.

"Have you remembered anything from last night?"

"Like what?"

He turned to face me, one arm up on the couch. I stared in awe as Cheeto circled Connor's feet and sat down, staring up at him. Then Besos followed.

Morely watched from his favorite spot above the TV.

The agent glanced at the animals sitting at his feet and looked back at me.

"Like anything."

I shrugged, trying not to notice how the animals reacted when he casually reached down to pet them. They acted like he was the Second Coming. I frowned, inexplicably annoyed.

"No. I mean, it was packed. Nothing stood out."

Shut up shut up shut up.

"You sure about that?"

I nodded slowly. I hated lying to anyone, even the law. But I didn't have a choice. I hugged myself, hoping no one saw him come in.

At least he didn't look like a stiff tonight.

"Here boy. Leave him alone. Cheeto! Besos!"

They ignored me but Connor quirked an eyebrow at me.

"Cheeto?"

"The cat. He's orange. Sorry, if they are bothering you, I can-"

"It's fine."

I chewed my lip. Then I blurted out the question that had been bothering me since he appeared at the door.

"Do you usually make house calls?"

He just stared at me.

"We have more photos to show you. I need to know who was there last night. We can do that here, or we can do it at headquarters."

"It's going to be hard to say with one hundred percent certainty. I don't interact with the customers all that much."

He gave me an odd look and then he smiled slowly.

"That's probably for the best."

"That's what Mason says."

He laughed and shook his head.

"I bet he does."

Rrrrrrr...

I realized Besos was growling. Even lazy, chubby Morely sat up and looked towards the kitchen. Cheeto sat up too.

For a minute I thought Mason had come home early. But Mase was a big guy and his boots made a lot of noise. I always knew when Mase was home.

I heard footsteps running away and the roar of a bike.

Yeah, definitely not Mason.

Connor pulled his gun and was on his feet in an instant.

"Someone is outside."

He held his hand out when I tried to follow him. I followed anyway.

He moved so fast and so silently that I almost missed it. The man was like a damn panther. Sneakier than a cat. I had a feeling he was a thousand times as deadly.

He paused and looked at me.

"Stay back."

He opened the door and stepped outside with his gun drawn. He swung around quickly, checking the walkway and the alley that led to the back.

Then he holstered his gun and stared at something on the ground.

"What the fuck is this?"

CONNOR

The roses were covered in blood.

An ex-boyfriend then. Or a stalker. *Or a threat.*

I stepped back and turned to face her, leaving the door open as I phoned it in. If it was related to the case I need it bagged and tagged.

"What is it?"

I cocked an eyebrow at her as I put my phone away.

"Someone left you a gift."

"Me?"

"I assume no one would send Mason two dozen red roses covered in blood."

"Blood?"

"Looks like it. You got an admirer? A crazy one?"

She shook her head but I saw the moment of hesitation. The moment when she was deciding what lie to tell me. How to spin it.

She knew something.

I could see it in her breathtaking eyes. The kaleidoscope of different shades of blue projected pure terror.

I felt it in my gut.

It made me furious. Who would threaten such a sweet, young girl? It suddenly didn't matter to me that she lived with a biker anymore. That she worked at the bar.

It was despicable.

From the beginning, I had a strong hunch who had been behind the murder. And I had a very good idea of who she was afraid of, even though she tried to hide it. I could see her fear. Taste it. And I also had a good idea of why.

Because she was mixed up in it, dammit.

I didn't care who she associated with. I only cared who she was. And I knew she was good. Not perfect, even though her looks were flawless. She was defensive and wounded and living in the wrong world.

But she was good.

I felt it in my gut. Deeper than that. I felt it in the part of me that I had forgotten existed. I felt it in my soul.

Fuck me.

She bent forward in the open doorway, reaching for the roses. I took her arm, guiding her back from the door.

"Don't touch it. Evidence, honey."

Her eyes were wide.

"Evidence?"

I nodded and stared as she tugged her hoodie shut over the lacy little thing she was wearing. I swallowed, not letting go of her arm. One strap was still visible where it rested on the creamy skin of her shoulder.

That sexy spaghetti strap top of hers was going to kill me. She looked so sweet and cuddly in that outfit. It was hard to think of her as the enemy. Hard to think about breaking her.

Using her to catch a killer.

But I had to. I knew I did. She was the only witness, even if she was pretending not to have a Goddamn clue.

She knew something.

The words kept circling in my head. There was no other reason to threaten her. No reason for her to be afraid. I was going to have to wait on forensics to tell me if there was any sign of who had done this. They would camp out in the front yard and comb through everything.

And that created a whole other problem. The one I'd been dreading. Hoping to somehow avoid.

Once they showed up word would get out that Casey was talking to the us. That looked bad, even though she was barely cooperating.

That was it. Game over.

Her life would be in jeopardy the moment I put in the call.

I stared at her, my jaw ticking. She was part of this officially now. On the books. But that didn't mean I wasn't going to do every damn thing I could to keep her safe.

Even if it meant bending the rules a little.

Or, a lot.

"Pack a bag. You're coming with me."

"What? No!"

I stepped closer and she backed away into the wall. I leaned over her, staring deep into her huge eyes. I wanted her to tell me the truth dammit!

"Tell me this wasn't Dante. Tell me you have a psychotic exboyfriend. Because from what I have found so far, you don't."

She stared at me, breathing fast. I nodded, taking her silence as a 'no.' So what if I'd admitted looking into her personal life, or lack thereof?

She didn't need to know how Goddamn happy it had made me to know she wasn't attached. Hell, it looked like she never had been.

The girl's online profile was devoid of boyfriends, past or present. No family photos either. It was devoid of almost anything except her dubious taste in reality television.

She liked the pages of almost every cheesy housewife show in existence.

It was set to private, but we had ways around that. It wasn't even hard. I could access her private messages if I wanted to. Her emails. Her texts.

I hadn't found one thing that indicted there a guy in her life. There was nothing. Other than her and Mason talking about the damn animals all the time.

I had run facial recognition software too. Searching to see if she had another name, or a hidden profile. A rap sheet. Overdue library books. Parking tickets.

Anything.

So far it had come up with zilch. No images of her on a milk carton, no Instagram pictures of her on someone's lap.

Of course, it was still processing. So I kept hoping something would come up. Because as far as I could tell, Casey Jones hadn't even existed until four years ago.

And that was going to complicate the case. And anything that came after.

Because for some crazy reason I couldn't imagine letting this girl out of my sight.

She clearly had other ideas. She glared up at me, clearly not intimidated by my closeness. I could smell her. I was inches away from her lips. From her delicious body.

"I don't need your protection."

"Yes, you fucking do."

I was close enough to kiss her. I was hard as a rock, just from standing there. I could feel heat and electricity jumping between our bodies.

She shook her head frantically.

"They'll kill him. If they think- if they think I know something."

I gripped her arm, but not hard. I stared at my hand where I held her, then back into her beautiful, panicked eyes.

"Don't you?"

She shook her head again but there was no conviction in it. We both knew she was lying. And we both knew she was in danger.

I let my eyes slide over her, resting on her tempting lips.

"It doesn't matter now. This place is going to be crawling with forensics soon. Even if you don't know something, it's going to look like you do."

She blinked and I smiled at her, trying to look reassuring. Now that I'd decided to take her with me, I felt better. I would keep her safe.

And I would catch the killer.

Then and only then would I decide what to do about this insane attraction I had for little Miss Casey not-her-real-name Jones.

"Get packed."

That stubborn little chin came up.

"I won't leave Mason."

"Mason can handle himself."

"I don't care. I owe him."

I pushed away from the wall and pulled my phone out.

"Fine. I will get him in custody too."

"No- wait!"

Her hands reached for me. I held perfectly still, barely breathing through the chain reaction that simple touch set off.

Her hand. My shoulder. Straight to my cock.

"Get packed or I will do it for you."

I shook her off and put the call in for someone to pay Mason a visit. He would get picked up and taken to a safe house. One set up by the agency.

Of course, I didn't mention to anyone that I was taking her.

Or *where* I was taking her. That was going to stay completely off the record. Nothing official about it.

Or legal.

She was coming home with me.

CASSANDRA

It would be okay. Everything would be okay. I'd made Connor promise.

And for some reason, I believed him.

Mason would be safe. Pissed off, but safe. Connor had even agreed to take all the animals to the safe house too.

But not the same safe house I was going to.

No one could know where we were going. I wasn't even allowed to take my phone. I sent one text before we left, with the agent watching me like a hawk the whole time.

I'm safe. Things just got complicated. I'm sorry.

I bit my lip, stealing a glance at Connor. He was staring out the window, my bags in his hands.

He looked grim. Furious. Determined.

Then he looked at me and nodded, his eyes softening immediately. Just like that, I felt safe. Or at least, safe-ish.

How crazy was that?

I curled up in the passenger seat as Connor drove me out of town. We drove in silence as we left the suburban streets and slid into the darkness of the countryside. The hills were getting steeper, the roads narrower. The headlights were fewer and farther in between.

For a moment, I realized that I was completely at his mercy. If he was a bad guy, this would be the end of the movie. Dump body in ditch, roll credits.

I grimaced. Maybe I watched a little *too* much reality TV. I especially loved those shows about people who had snapped and committed grisly murders.

Mostly scorned women. Those were the best. Sometimes you even cheered for them.

Well, sometimes.

Yeah, I loved all those true crime shows. Though after this, if I survived, I doubted I would enjoy them anymore.

"So, are you in school or anything?"

I snapped back to the present. I swallowed and shook my head.

"Next Fall. I was supposed to start then."

College already felt like something that had been derailed. I was probably not going to be here in the Fall. Hopefully I would still be alive, but everything else felt like a longshot.

"College?"

I nodded and realized he couldn't see me in the dark. Brilliant Cass.

"Yeah. I mean, I always wanted to become a veterinarian but I know that takes a really long time."

"An M.D.? No shit?"

I shrugged.

"I really like animals. I'm not too squeamish either…"

I trailed off, realizing I was a lot more squeamish than I once thought. What I'd seen the other night had cleared that up right quick. I felt a little sick as my mind replayed the sound of that knife sliding through skin…

"That's really cool. You got really high scores on your GED so it should be easy for you."

I stared at him.

"How do you know that?"

He gave me a look and didn't answer. I felt naked suddenly. He'd looked me up obviously. Not just to see if I had a criminal record.

That made me feel… weird.

I crossed my arms, determined not to let him see me squirm.

"What else did you find out?"

"Well, for starters, Casey Jones isn't your real name."

My mouth dropped open and went dry.

"And you watch a lot of really questionable television."

I bit my lip, realizing how vulnerable I really was. He was right. Casey Jones was a fake name. It wasn't legally mine. I didn't even exist on paper.

It's not like I'd done anything wrong when I'd run off. At least I hoped my old foster mom hadn't accused me of anything illegal... not that I'd done anything but run off.

Either way I was of age now. It's not like they could make me go back.

There was nothing to be afraid of.

I jumped as a hand landed on my shoulder.

"Hey relax, you aren't under investigation."

"Then why did you investigate me?"

He cleared his throat, his eyes on the road.

"I was curious. Occupational hazard."

I looked out the window at the trees. I had no idea what to say about that. Why would he be curious about me?

I was a waitress in a biker bar. I was no one special. I was a teenage runaway who had managed to avoid selling her body to survive. And that was just dumb luck.

"We're here."

I rolled down the window as he turned off the main road. I heard rattling as he took a gravel road up through the trees. I didn't see any lights or a house.

Yeah... this was a good place to dump a body.

I glanced at Connor but he didn't look at me. And I didn't get a serial killer vibe. And I highly doubted he worked for Dante.

And Dante hadn't said he wanted to kill me yet. Not exactly. Not yet anyway. It was probably his idea of a romantic gesture to send me bloody roses.

Connor had a strange smile on his face when we finally pulled up to a log cabin ten minutes later. We were far from the main road, if you could call it that. We were pretty much far from *anywhere*.

I got out of the car and stared up at the welcoming front porch. It was a real log cabin. The sort mountain men lived in on TV.

My God, we really were in the middle of nowhere.

"What is this place?"

He looked at me and smiled the slightest bit.

"Home."

CONNOR

"**H**ome?"

I nodded and went to the trunk to get her bags. The girl travelled light, even with the heat I'd put on her ass to get ready fast. A small duffle with some clothes and a backpack with some books and toiletries. That was it.

A word flashed in my mind, sharp and immediately recognizable as true.

Runaway.

That must be what it was. What she was. Casey had packed fast. Like she was used to running. I looked at her in the darkness, the defensive posture, the sense of aloneness…

That was it. Everything clicked into place.

She was a runaway. And somehow, Mason had saved her.

For once in my life, I had a reason to really respect a criminal. Because he'd done right by this one girl. I slammed the trunk shut and she jumped.

"It's okay. You're safe here."

She looked up at me as I came to stand beside her. The moon was bright and I could see every inch, every graceful curve of her face.

"No one is ever really safe."

I wanted to yank her against me and hold her. To tell her she was wrong. Even if I knew she was right.

What did safe mean anyway? Danny wasn't safe, even with me looking after him. Danny was gone.

I clenched my jaw. *Eyes on the prize, DeWitt.* Solve the crime first.

Then you can decide what to do about the girl.

"Come on, let me get you settled."

She waited outside on the porch while I turned the lights on. I showed her to the guest room on the second floor. I was down the hall from her, and closer to the stairs. That way I would hear her if she tried to sneak out.

Or if anyone tried to get in.

"Are you tired?"

She shook her head.

"I slept all day."

I smiled a little.

"I did too."

We went downstairs and I offered her food. She said no, but she did take a glass of water. She sat on the couch, looking like a bird about to take flight.

"Have you heard about Mason?"

"Not yet."

She chewed on that soft, sexy bottom lip of hers. I stared at her hungrily, desperate to have a taste. She noticed the TV and perked up a bit.

"Do you have cable?"

I picked up the remote and tossed it to her.

"Knock yourself out."

CASSANDRA

The man never stopped working. He was out on the porch, his voice low as he took call after call. He paced back and forth.

Every once in a while, he came in and used the laptop at the kitchen table. Then his phone would buzz and he'd leave again.

It kind of felt domestic. Like when Mason was working on his bike and I would sit outside with a book. It felt oddly... normal. Which was odd in itself.

Never mind the fact that I was on lockdown and Dante had sent me twenty-four blood soaked long-stemmed roses.

I wondered for the hundredth time why he hadn't just killed me then and there. It would have been quick. I was short and he was tall and strong. I doubt I would have even had time to scream.

But he hadn't. And now I pretty much had no choice but to run. Run, or squeal. Or both.

My ass was going to end up in witness protection if I was willing to talk. I needed to talk to Mason. I'd tried to keep him out of it and now it was too late.

So run from Dante and the law or witness protection. That's *if* I was lucky. If I was unlucky, I'd just be dead.

I sighed and flipped the channel again. Commercials, man. I hated them. If I lived here, this show would have been taped and I could fast forward through it.

Of course as of now, I didn't live anywhere. Mason's place was under surveillance, by the FBI *and* the Raisers.

I could just disappear and save them all the trouble. I had a feeling that Mason would come after me if I did.

Never mind the Boy Scout outside.

He seemed like the type who didn't let go of stuff too easy. Of course, I didn't really know him. But I usually got a good sense of people, and that's one of the things I was picking up from him.

I'd been watching TV for over an hour. I'd seen various housewives and half a show about people working at a hotel that I'd never seen before.

Basically, they were all good looking idiots.

And I freaking loved it.

I settled back into the cushions. It was a good couch. Worn in enough to be incredibly comfy. It smelled nice too. The whole place was scruffy but clean and kind of cool in an old school way.

Kind of like Connor.

He came back inside and reached into the fridge. He pulled out a beer, looked at me, and put it back.

"Go ahead, I don't mind."

He shrugged and pulled it out again, twisting the top off the bottle. I noticed he didn't offer me one. Probably because I was technically underage.

"You really live here?"

He leaned against a post and stared at me, taking a swig. He was so serious. I couldn't help but wonder what he was thinking about. What made him tick.

Doesn't matter, Cass. Escape plan. Mason. Plausible lies.

"Yeah. I really do."

"Do you usually take witnesses here?"

"No."

"So... why am I here again?"

He drank again and wiped the back of his mouth.

"I had to get you out of there. It would have taken hours to get something set up. Would you rather be waiting in an interrogation room until dawn again?"

I shook my head, sliding my hands underneath my legs. He'd brought me here to be kind. He may have even broken rules to do it.

"Did they find out anything about the roses?"

He nodded slowly.

"It was chicken blood. That's what you were asking, right?"

"Yes. And if they knew... who sent it?"

"No." He took another slow sip of his beer. He never took his eyes off me. "But you know."

I stared at the ground. My heart beating hard and fast. I stood up abruptly and turned off the TV.

"I think I'll go to bed-"

He grabbed me as I passed him. He spun me so that my back was against the post. He leaned over me and stared at me like I was something delicate and rare.

His fingers brushed my face.

I held my breath as the world seemed to stop.

Then he stepped back. Slowly, so slowly, I slid away from the post. I forced myself to take one step and then another until I was up the stairs.

Only when I was in the guest room could I breath normally again.

I got into the bed he'd made up for me and stared out the one window. I could see the stars above the tree line. I was still awake when I heard him come upstairs a few hours later.

His footsteps paused outside my door. That's when I knew I wasn't imagining what had happened in the living room.

What had *almost* happened.

Connor had almost kissed me.

CONNOR

This was hell. Pure torture. I rolled over in my big, empty bed, my rock hard cock pressing uselessly into the mattress.

I had never wanted a woman in my bed this badly before.

I had never wanted *anything* this badly before.

And that scared the shit out of me.

I was already in danger of getting in trouble for this. Career-ending trouble. It wasn't even on the books. I'd just... taken her with me.

She should be in a safe house like Mason. Not the same one. I needed to keep them separated.

You're doing it for Danny.

Lie.

This is the best way to break her.

Another lie.

You will break her.

Truth.

I knew I could break her. She was tough but she was just a girl. I was a trained federal agent. I could wear her down and make her talk. No matter how brave she was.

But at what cost? The thought that I'd put her in danger was already tearing me up inside. Now I was going to work her over emotionally too? Make her think she had even worse things to worry about from me?

I wasn't sure I could do it and look in the mirror afterwards. But I had to do it. I owed it to my partner's memory.

I moaned and closed my eyes.

She was so close... her soft, warm body laying less than twenty feet away. I could just give in to temptation. It would be so easy. I knew just what I would do.

I'd wake her with a soft kiss, then let my hands run over her body. I'd sink into the bed, twisting and turning until I was between her thighs.

Then I would go to town. Unleash everything I had on her. All the years alone. All the heat she seemed to stir up in me.

Too much heat.

I gave in, knowing I wasn't getting any sleep tonight. I needed to cool down. I opened the window and stared out of it. It's a good thing I did.

Because I could see her running away.

A furtive movement by the tree line caught my eye.

I blinked. Yes, that was Casey. She was actually trying to get away from me. I ran for the stairs, practically taking them in one leap.

How the fuck was I supposed to protect her if she ran? I grabbed a flashlight as I ran out the front door, not caring that I was shirtless and shoeless.

She'd been headed for the road from what I could tell. I ran at full speed, my eyes scanning the darkness. There. I thought I saw something just ahead-

I smiled grimly as I saw her tip toeing down the dirt road, looking utterly lost. Not on my watch sweetheart. I was going to have to take drastic measures apparently.

I reached out and closed my hand over her shoulder. I ignored the electricity that leapt between us. I was too angry to care how scared she looked.

Gotcha.

CASSANDRA

"You have got to be fucking kidding me."

Connor's hand came down on my shoulder, hard. He spun me around and I stared at him in surprise.

How the hell had he heard me? I was quiet as hell. It was one of my special skills, dammit.

"What do you think you are doing?"

My mouth opened but no sound came out. He rolled his eyes and the next thing I knew I was slung over his shoulder and being carried swiftly back up the hill.

He carried me and all my stuff with ease. I could see that his feet were bare. It was pretty cold out here and he wasn't wearing a shirt or shoes.

I winced, realizing he was more than a little bit pissed.

And he kind of had a right to be.

I was distracted by his body. I'd never been this close to a half-naked man before. Especially not one that looked like Connor. My body pressed against his bare skin. His bare, hot, silky skin. His hot skin that covered all those massive muscles.

His many, many muscles.

I had to steady myself with my hands on his chest. And lower. One hand settled against his flat stomach as I held on for dear life.

His hand shifted on my lower back and he grunted. It was like I was a log being carried by a lumberjack. Or a wild animal. He just hoisted me up and took me away.

It was overwhelming.

It was also kind of insanely sexy.

And that was before I realized I could smell him. Just a hint of something warm and masculine, along with all this fresh woodsy air.

No wonder he smelled like the trees.

He stomped up the porch stairs and kicked the door open. Then he kicked the door shut again and dropped me onto the couch.

He pointed a finger at me.

"Don't say a fucking word."

I sat there, feeling like an ass. Who gets caught sneaking out? And where the hell had I thought I was going anyway?

Now Connor was angry and I was at his mercy. Well, still at his mercy. I was pretty much screwed on all fronts and we both knew it.

I watched as he made a pot of coffee, ignoring me completely. He stared at me while it dripped, his arms crossed over that massive, bare chest of his. I swallowed nervously and looked away.

He rattled around some, and I heard a drill. I thought he was securing the door. That wouldn't stop me from running again.

Clearly he didn't realize I had gone out through the window.

A few minutes later, a cup of coffee with cream and sugar appeared in front of me. I stared at it, my mind turning. He must have remembered how I liked it.

That was… sweet.

"Drink."

I took the cup and had a sip. At the moment, I would have done anything he asked of me.

"Talk."

I exhaled and looked at him. Somehow the warmth in my hands was giving me courage. Then the ferocious look in his eyes instantly depleted it again.

I was at 50% on the brave-o-meter, at most.

"I need to see Mason."

His jaw ticked.

"He's safe."

"He's in a safe house?"

"I didn't say that."

"He refused to go in didn't he?"

He stared at me. Then he nodded abruptly.

"I need to talk to him."

He walked over to the couch and leaned forward until his arms were braced on either side of my head. He stared at me, his eyes hard and unforgiving.

"Absolutely fucking not."

We stared at each other and I realized he didn't want to kiss me now. He wanted to throttle me maybe. Or spank me.

He ran his hands through his hair and sighed.

"I'm trying to keep you safe Casey. I couldn't take you to a safe house unless you were willing to talk. No one knows you are here."

"What?"

"You aren't a witness until you talk. So talk."

"Why did you say you were taking Mason to a safe house then?"

"I tried. There is some wiggle room. And with you gone, it seemed like maybe he was gonna crack-"

"You used me!"

He smiled at me.

"Honey, I will use anyone and anything to get to Dante. I am trying to keep you alive though."

"For the case."

He stared at me.

"For the case."

"I want fucking out of here. Now."

He shook his head and reached out his hand.

"Give me your ankle."

He held up a chain and smiled at me.

"What? No!"

"I need sleep and you need to stay put. So I repeat, give me your ankle."

I shook my head.

"Unless you want to be handcuffed to me? We could sleep in the same bed."

My heart thudded and I felt an odd warmth in my center. Between my legs.

I swallowed and shook my head.

"Didn't think so."

Was it my imagination or did he look disappointed?

He grabbed my leg and snapped the cuff into place. I kicked and screamed but it was no use. He held the chain up and showed me where it attached to the post.

It was long enough to get to the kitchen or the bathroom. I stared at he started removing anything that could be used as a weapon from the drawers.

That bastard had thought of everything! Now I was truly fucked. I couldn't leave and I couldn't defend myself.

I tugged on the cuff around my ankle and screamed.

CONNOR

"Scream all you want, honey. No one's gonna hear you."

She tugged frantically at her ankle, then stopped to glare at me. Dammit, the old stereotype was true. Casey was even prettier than usual when she was angry.

"You're not going anywhere."

"You can't do this."

"I can. And I will."

"This is- kidnapping!"

"You aren't a kid. And I'm a federal agent."

"Good! If someone finds out they will throw you in jail!"

I smiled at her calmly, my eyes trailing over her long legs. She was wearing tight jeans and they were extremely sexy for some reason.

Probably because she was wearing them.

"I don't think so."

"Oh yeah? How are you going to explain this?"

She held up the chain and waved it at me.

"Kinky sex game?"

Her mouth opened in shock. I had her there. And damn if it didn't give me ideas.

"I'm tired Casey, or whatever your name is. But you are going to tell me something. You are going to tell me *everything*."

Her eyes were wide as I walked over to the couch and sat down next to her.

"No, I'm not."

"Yes. You are."

I smiled and reached out for her. Then I pulled her over my lap. She screamed as she lay facedown on the couch. Her perfect bottom was high up in the air as she wiggled around, trying to get away.

I grunted, realizing my dick was getting hard and that there was no way to hide it from her.

She stopped wiggling with a loud gasp.

Oh yeah, she'd noticed alright.

I rested one hand on her back to hold her in place and laid one over the generous globes of her delicious looking ass.

Hmmff... it felt nice too. Really fucking nice. I smiled to myself and lifted my hand.

Time to make it jiggle.

SMACK.

"Was Dante at the Jar that night?"

"Ow! Yes, Christ I told you!"

SMACK.

"Did you see him with the vic?"

Silence. So be it. I lifted my hand again.

SMACK.

"Did you see Dante with the vic?"

"No!"

I stopped, my hand frozen in midair. I knew it was insane what I was doing. Everything I was doing.

I was too close to the case. It was the middle of the night. The girl brought out a protective urge in me.

But it was more than all that.

Her shoulders were shaking. I let my hand rest on her bottom. I stroked her softly, knowing that it was dangerous.

Stupid.

But Jesus it felt right.

She sat up and stared at me. Those bright blue eyes of hers shimmered with unshed tears.

I reached out, my head tilted as I examined her. My fingers found her cheek and noticed that they were dry. She hadn't let a single tear fall.

I smiled into that beautiful, perfect face of hers.

"Liar."

CASSANDRA

"I'm- I'm not lying."

He shook his head slowly, his fingers still cupping my cheek. We'd crossed all kinds of lines in the past ten minutes.

Maybe we'd been crossing them since we met.

The man had me chained up and had spanked me like a child. But in that moment, I knew he was trying to keep me safe.

I felt safe.

And that wasn't the weirdest thing at all. The weirdest thing, was that I wanted him to kiss me.

I wondered if I had that syndrome when people fall in love with their captors.

Stockholm Syndrome.

But I'd only technically been captured for twenty minutes. So... unlikely. Besides, what I was feeling wasn't love. It couldn't be.

But I did seem to be devloping one hell of a crush on Connor DeWitt.

And I had a suspicion the feeling was mutual. Which made everything even more confusing. He was trying to protect me. He hadn't kissed me, even though it seemed like he wanted to.

He wasn't a guy trying to bang the waitress from The Jar with the bright blue eyes. Or maybe he was. But it didn't feel like that.

Besides, he wasn't making any moves on me.

In that moment, I almost wished that he would.

He swallowed and I stared at his Adam's apple as it bobbed up and down. I had an urge to run my fingers over it. Feel the roughness of his stubble.

He stood up and I suddenly felt shockingly alone. He walked around the room, turning the lights down. He brought me a glass of water and a blanket.

Then he took his laptop and the box of sharp objects he'd confiscated earlier. He stood at the foot of the stairs, watching me. His finger brushed the light switch on the wall and the room plunged into darkness.

"Get some sleep."

CONNOR

'What the fuck are you doing DeWitt?'

I could hear Danny in my head. I could almost see him leaning against the dresser, giving me a dark look. He sounded worried, which was a bad sign. Usually he liked the off the wall stuff.

He was the one always telling me to loosen up. Have fun. Let the chips fall where they may.

Well, the chips had gotten him killed and now I was in the middle of throwing my career away for revenge, and a barely legal girl. I had to admit that to myself now. I wasn't just using her to get answers.

I was doing something else entirely. What exactly, I had no fucking idea.

I sprawled out on the bed and stared out the window. Dawn was just beginning to light up the sky.

'Well, let's see Danny. I have a girl chained up in my living room. I just spanked her. But what I'd really like to do is chain her to my bed.'

Then I could fuck the truth out of her. Make her scream my name. Maybe tell me the damn truth as I toyed with her gorgeous body, teasing and touching and tasting her at will.

I had a feeling little Miss Jones was absofuckinglutely delicious.

I wouldn't even fuck her for a good long while. I'd take my time, feasting on every inch of her.

Fuck. I hadn't been this hard since- well, ever.

I rolled onto my stomach and moaned as my cock rubbed against the mattress. Maybe I should just take care of this myself-

But it felt wrong. She was right there. I wanted the real thing, not just a mindless release.

An empty release, without the object of my twisted affections being involved.

I was inches away from walking down the stairs, pulling off my clothes and doing something unthinkable.

The girl is chained up, DeWitt. Don't be a creep. This is starting to feel like *Silence of The fucking Lambs.*

My phone pinged and I stared at the screen. My hand was already wrapped around my shaft. I released my grip and picked up the phone instead.

Saved by the bell. Literally.

I stared at the phone and sat up.

Fuck me.

They'd found another body. At The Jar. And this time, Mason was a suspect.

CASSANDRA

I woke up to the smell of pancakes. I blinked and sat up, rubbing my eyes. Connor was in the kitchen, cooking something.

Pancakes most likely. Real smart, Cass. Putting two and two together like that.

I eyeballed Connor warily. He looked sharp, like he was going somewhere. He was fully dressed in a similar outfit to the night he'd come into The Jar. Suit jacket and jeans. He was even wearing his gun.

And an apron.

The combination of the gray flannel suit jacket and the plaid apron was almost too much. I would have laughed but the way I felt when I looked at him made me nervous.

Not because he was scary.

Because I liked looking at him so much.

Too much.

Not to mention the clanking sound when my feet hit the floor made him give me a look that made my insides turn to jelly.

Oh right, he'd chained me up. Great.

He might be hot, but he was also possibly psychotic. And I had zero options at this point. I could try and be nice. Or I could try and get away again.

With a hacksaw maybe.

"Here. Eat."

He put a cup of coffee in front of me, along with a plate of pancakes. He'd already put a neat little pat of butter on top. And syrup.

Not too much, either. It was pretty much a perfect plate. I stared at it, my mouth watering.

"I have to go out."

I realized I was starving as I reached for the food and immediately started cutting it into neat squares. I stopped long enough to ask him a question before popping a big, juicy bite of pancake into my mouth.

Damn, the guy could cook.

"Great. When does this come off?"

I wagged my foot at him and he stared at it, clearing his throat. I noticed his eyes lingered on my bare foot and lowered it with a clank.

"It doesn't."

"You're leaving me here chained up? What if the building catches fire?"

"It won't."

"But-"

"Eat. Rest. Read a book. I'll be back in a few hours."

He nodded and I saw he had brought my stuff down. He'd even set out a couple of books on the coffee table and a neatly stacked change of clothes rested at the foot of the couch.

My eyes got wide when I saw the fresh white cotton bra and panties on top. Hello. He'd touched my panties.

His gaze followed mine and we both stared at those small white panties with the pink bow. I saw his lips open slightly. He licked his lips too. Like he was hungry.

Well, he should have some pancakes if he was hungry! Not go through my fucking bags! I sighed and held up the chain.

"How can I change with this on?"

His jaw ticked. He sighed and glanced at his watch.

"Fine. You can change real quick. No time for a shower."

He pulled a key from his pocket and unlocked my ankle cuff. I shivered from the warm, rough feeling of his hands on my skin. The man's callouses had callouses.

It didn't hurt or scratch my skin though. It kinda tickled.

He sat back and raised his eyebrows.

"Well, go ahead."

I grabbed the clothes and ran for the bathroom. I half expected him to stop me. To tell me to change in front of him. To make sure I wasn't hiding a weapon.

Or a bobby pin... Too bad I didn't wear my hair in an updo or something. Not that I was good at picking locks. But I did know how.

Note to self: next time you plan to get kidnapped, put your hair in French twist.

My hands fumbled with my clothes, grabbing a washcloth to clean my face with cold water. I rubbed the damp cloth under my arms and between my legs before throwing the clothes on.

I had this crazy feeling he was going to break the door down at any second.

When I came back out, he was on the couch, thumbing through one of my books. It was a racy romance novel that I'd read half a dozen times. I flushed and grabbed for it.

His fingers brushed mine and I gasped as our eyes met. He was smiling at me knowingly. Like he knew all my secrets.

I yanked the book out of his hand and glared at him. He held up the cuff and I rolled my eyes. But I lifted my foot all the same. He never broke eye contact as he reached out and grabbed it.

He rested my foot on his knee and gently pushed my jeans up. Then he blew on the skin and I shivered.

He mumbled 'better if the skin is dry' as he fit the shackle into place and locked it.

There. I was trapped. Again. And I'd willing participated in it this time. Semi-willingly anyway.

Why did I feel so safe then?

I sat down on the couch, realizing I was going to be stuck here alone and bored. He cleared his throat and set down a cellphone.

"I will text or call. You will answer."

He smiled.

"It does not call out. It does not text out. It only receives. So don't even think about it."

I leaned back with a huff, refusing to look at him.

"Just in case you get hungry I made you a sandwich. Two actually. There is juice and soda in the fridge."

My mouth dropped, staring at him as he stood to adjust his weapon and make sure he had his badge.

"Exactly how long are you going to be gone?"

"It could be a while." He grinned and gestured to the book. "You have plenty of stuff to distract you while you eagerly wait for me to get back."

"Eagerly?"

I chucked the book at him and he caught it.

"Maybe I'll take it with me." He gave me a long assessing look. "I could use the tips."

My mouth dropped open. He could use... wait, what?

He slid the book into his jacket pocket. He never stopped looking at me as he licked his lips. I blinked as he shook his head and pursed his lips.

"Stay out of trouble."

And then he was gone.

CONNOR

Those panties. Dear God in Heaven. Those sweet, sexy little white panties.

I'd taken my time going through her things, letting her sleep. It was still early but I was expected at the agency. I needed to hustle.

But I had taken my time with those panties. I'd folded all her clothes neatly. Even the underthings.

Especially her underthings.

Those I had folded twice.

I'd laid them flat on the bed, running my hands over them. Imagining her soft little pussy underneath. I was hard and aching as I laid them gently on top of the stack of clean clothes.

I had resisted the urge to sniff them. Barely.

Try not to be a total fucking creep, DeWitt.

I patted the book in my pocket. My witness had a dirty mind it seemed. Or she was curious about sex, at the very least.

I'd be more than happy to instruct her…

I groaned and adjusted my package. Great. Another day with an unrelenting hard on.

Just what the doctor ordered. *Not.* If the doctor had any feelings, he would prescribe twenty-four hours in bed with my little runaway.

Longer. A week. A month. But twenty-four hours was a good start.

At this point, I would take what I could get. Literally. Panties. Books. Anything.

I pulled into The Jar and closed my eyes. I knew Mason was inside, probably frothing at the mouth. Worse than that, Casey was going to freak when she found out what had happened.

Another Hell Raiser body. But this time, her guardian *was* a suspect. Lighting never strikes twice in my experience. And when it does, its a sign of something bad.

I walked inside and saw him immediately. He was cuffed and sitting at one of the tables, fuming while the place was scoured top to bottom by forensics.

Yellow tape was everywhere. Fingerprinting was useless but they were taking some samples. The place was pretty much overrun with federal agents.

The Jar would definitely not be opening anytime soon.

Mason glared at me as I walked over to him. I smiled, pulling out the chair across the table. I didn't beat around the bush. If he knew something, or if he knew how to get to her, then I was going to use that as leverage.

Use them against each other.

"Someone's setting you up, aren't they?"

He grit his teeth and bared them at me. It was easy to forget with his good looks and whiskey warm voice, but Mason *was* an Untouchable. He used to ride with the wildest of them.

"It's because of her, isn't it?"

"What the fuck have you done with her, DeWitt? If you touch her-"

I smiled at him and popped a stick of gum into my mouth. Let him think I'd touched her. I sure as hell wanted to.

"She's safe. You on the other hand..."

He spat on the ground. I couldn't say I blamed him for being pissed. All the signs pointed to another Untouchable, or Hell Raiser, being behind the crimes.

But circumstantially... it was not looking good for old Mase.

I paused, realizing I'd picked up Casey's nickname for the biker. Who wasn't all that much older than me.

Jesus, maybe I *was* a dirty old man. I'd thought about pocketing those panties after all... she had a couple of pairs.

I decided I would be happy to buy her some more. Lots of pairs of fresh little underwear. Enough that she wouldn't notice if one went missing.

"We need to talk." I leaned back and shook my head. "She saw something."

"She tell you that?"

"What do you think?"

He smirked for a minute, then the smile fell.

"Fuck."

I nodded.

"Yeah, fuck."

We sat there in silence for a few minutes.

"I'm trying to keep her safe. To do that, I need to keep you safe."

I tilted my head.

"Oh and the pets. Cheeto and- well whatever other ones."

He laughed and shook his head.

"She'll never squeal. It's the only reason she's alive."

"I know she won't." I smiled. "But you will."

"What the fuck are you up to, DeWitt?"

"Please, call me Connor. We're about to get real friendly."

He groaned and leaned back in his chair.

"You're going to get us all killed man."

"I'm trying not to. No one knows where she is. If you talk *for* her, maybe we can leave her out of it altogether."

He stared at me.

"You touch her, Connor? I know you want to."

I raised a brow and nodded once. What was the point in lying about that? I wanted to touch her. Jesus Christ, did I ever.

"If you hurt her, I will fucking cut your nuts off."

I made a tsking sound.

"Threatening a federal officer is never a good idea." I popped another stick of gum in my mouth. "Anyway, there are so many reasons to 'touch' a person in custody. Searching them. Restraining them. Holding them down."

I was pretty sure I saw actual steam come out of Mason's ears. So what if what I was proposing was stretching the rules? It would keep Casey out of it and get the bad guys. That was good enough to me.

"If you fuck her- if you hurt her-"

"Hey now!" I smiled at him as he struggled to get out of his chair. "I never kiss and tell."

Then I walked away to let him stew.

CASSANDRA

I stared at the ceiling, clicking through channels without even looking. It had been a few hours since Connor left me here, chained up like a dog. I'd already eaten all my pancakes and a sandwich.

Jesus, I was bored.

I couldn't stop worrying about Mase either. If he got killed because of me... I'd never forgive myself. If I talked they would kill him. But they might do it anyway, just to be on the safe side.

Connor kept telling me he would keep us both safe, but how could he be sure?

I sat up abruptly. Maybe he'd missed something. Maybe I could still get away... get to Mase.

Do something.

I started my search in the kitchen. As predicted, he'd taken everything sharp or pokey. Even the forks. Plenty of spoons though, in case I needed a weapon.

I pocketed one. A girl could do a lot of damage with a spoon.

I kept searching.

119

Jesus, the guy had a lot of weird stuff. Mallets for tenderizing. Old, milky white glass casserole pans. Jelly molds.

I looked around, realizing a lot of this stuff probably wasn't his. It was retro stuff, like you saw Betty Draper using on Mad Men. Maybe it had all been here when he moved in.

Either that, or he'd had a wife at some point. I shook my head. Connor didn't read that way to me.

There was something too... lone wolf about him.

I riffled around in the top cabinets next. I opened the one over the fridge and smiled.

Bingo.

Connor had quite a collection of fancy looking booze. I pulled down a bottle of fine tequila. Well, if nothing else, I could get drunk.

Great idea Cass. Really smart.

Still, mindlessly drinking myself into a stupor had an appeal t the moment. I'd only ever drank heavily a handful of times, but I had a beer and a shot now and then.

I mean, i might be technically underage by a few months but I worked in a biker bar for goodness sake.

I set the bottle down on the butcher block island and kept looking. I felt along the edges of cabinets and under the fridge.

I rubbed my fingers together, frowning as I stared at them.

Clean. No dust. No grime. Not even under the fridge.

I looked at the shiny chain on my leg and then at my fingers. What kind of man kept his house this clean. Jesus. Maybe Connor *was* a serial killer...

There was something so... Dexter about the cleanliness of the place.

No Cass. Not every clean freak is a murderer. Besides, the FBI probably ran profiles on their agents. They would know if he was chaining up young waitresses, fattening them up and eating them.

Right?

I shook my head and took a pull of the tequila, suddenly feeling like I needed a drink after all. I grabbed a lemon from the fridge and washed it. Then I stared at it and started laughing.

The damn thing might as well have been on the moon. Conn had taken all the sharp objects. He'd been alarmingly thorough about it.

How the hell was I supposed to cut a lemon with a spoon?

The man hadn't left so much as a butter knife behind. I rolled my eyes and took another swig from the bottle. It burned, but I felt myself seeing the humor in the situation suddenly.

I was trapped. Dante was after Mase and me. I was annoyingly fascinated with an FBI agent who had chained me to his wall.

And not for any kinky sex reasons unfortunately.

But here I was worried about lemons to chase my tequila. I sighed and crossed the room to the long, low wood cabinet under the TV. I pulled the cabinet doors open and stared. Boxes were everywhere.

Snooping really should be beneath me. But I was curious. And unfairly trapped here bored to tears. Besides, there must be something worthwhile in here…

I plopped on the floor with the bottle of booze and opened one. *Fuck me.* Rows of bullets shone dully in the afternoon light. I shoved it back and wiped my hands off.

Nope nope nope nope.

Okay, deep breath Cass. So what if the guy had a lot of ammo laying around? I knew he carried. I had a very healthy fear of guns, but a bullet couldn't hurt you if it was just sitting in a box.

I squinched up my face and reached for another box. This one had a fancy leather skin and a latch. I opened it and let out a soft '*oooo…*'

A poker set. Vintage from the looks of it. Rows of richly colored chips and several pristine decks of cards. Dice too.

One thing Mason had taught me to do, and do well, was gamble. We gambled for chores. We gambled for snacks. We gambled for pennies.

I had a knack for it. An ungodly talent, Mase said. That was after I won all the peanuts and snacks the first night I ever played.

I grinned. Maybe I'd get Connor to play me. I set the case on top of the cabinet and reached inside for another box. This one was cardboard.

I opened it and froze.

A badge was in here. A shirt. Photos and papers and-

Wow, Connor was ridiculously adorable when he was younger. Not that he wasn't even dishier now. Manlier somehow.

I sighed wistfully and sifted through the photos.

In the photos he was around my age, standing with a group of guys, looking like they were ready to take on the world. They all had hats that said 'FBI'.

Trainees, from the looks of it.

Connor looked so eager and excited to be there. His stunning eyes were shining in the pictures as I flipped through them. There was one guy in almost every one of the shots. It was clear the guy was Connor's best friend.

The guy had sandy blond hair and laughing eyes. In one picture he was wearing a balloon hat. I laughed

at the look on Connor's face in the photo. He looked embarrassed and fond and amused at the same time.

There were pictures of them graduating and out getting drunk and at barbecues. Regular life stuff. Then I got to the bottom of the box. No more pictures. Just a manilla folder.

I lifted the folder and the contents slid out. Papers that looked like an official report. And pictures. An obituary clipping.

I stared at the pictures. It was the same guy. Except in these pictures he was dead. He was pale and covered in blood and what looked like…. bullet holes.

I dropped the folder and scooted back, my hand over my mouth.

Connor's partner had died. He'd been killed. No wonder… well, Connor's steel like determination suddenly made sense.

And the deep sadness I could feel in him. The loneliness. His friend had died. His partner. I knew how it felt to lose the only ones you loved.

I stared at the scattered papers and swallowed, realizing this was something I shouldn't be looking at. Something I shouldn't see.

Slowly, and carefully, I started to put the box back together.

CONNOR

My foot felt heavy. Like lead. I wanted to put the pedal to the metal.

For once in my life, I was more than eager to get home. I'd run a couple of errands on the way back from headquarters. Now I was practically chomping at the bit to surprise her.

I dialed the dummy cell I'd left for Casey and tapped my fingers on the steering wheel.

"Hello?!"

I winced. She was shouting over some loud music.

"What are you doing?"

She giggled. Actually giggled.

"Hey, you. Did you see Mason?"

"Yes. He's fine." Well, relatively speaking. He was in custody under suspicion of murder. But I would tell her that later, when I could use it to my advantage.

I frowned, as a new song came on. She was playing dance music in the background. "What are you doing?"

"I found your stash!"

I groaned. What stash? Had she got out?

"What are you talking about?"

She giggled and hung up.

Casey had never so much as smiled since I'd met her. Not once. Let alone giggled like a schoolgirl. She was the most serious, not to mention the hottest, girl I'd ever met.

Or maybe you would think so, if you only met her at crime scenes and interrogation rooms.

She must have gotten out. She was at a party. At a friends house. Or with a boyfriend...

Dammit!

Her sexy little ass better be in the cabin. If not, I had tracking on the phone. At least I knew she had the phone with her.

But I had to get home first to drop everything off and log in to check her location. I pushed the speed limit, knowing my unmarked car would be recognizable to other law enforcement.

I went close to ninety the entire way, and was there in half the time it usually took. I stood outside, realizing she was not only home, but she was having a little party.

A very little party.

I stifled a grin when I saw the lights on and heard the music from inside. Whatever she was doing, she hadn't gotten out.

I was more than curious about what she was up to. I was intrigued.

More than anything, I wanted to hear her giggle like that in person.

I hoisted the bags out of the trunk and left the windows in the back open a crack. I'd be back out in a second. But first-

I peered in the window and froze, my eyes feasting on the girl dancing in my living room. Her body moved with perfect rhythm to the dance music she was blasting on my stereo.

Holy hell, the girl could dance.

She looked like she was in a music video. Her moves were somehow loose and precise at the same time. She was girlishly innocent and yet incredibly seductive.

And just like that, Mr. Boner was back in town.

I wondered what the hell had her in such a good mood. I opened the door. And then I saw it.

What a naughty girl. She had indeed found my stash. My little runaway was drinking my $50 bottle of tequila.

And I wasn't even mad about it.

I walked over to the radio and turned it off. As much as I was enjoying the show, I needed to get her attention.

"You know, it's illegal to drink at your age."

She laughed and smiled at me. My breath caught in my throat. Something was different.

Casey Jones was smiling at me like she meant it.

"Hi."

I set the bags down on the coffee table. Next to the half empty bottle of tequila. It was a good thing I had another bottle up there.

I was feeling pretty thirsty myself.

"Hi." I cleared my throat. "How much of this have you had?"

She shrugged.

"I don't know. I've just been sipping it."

"Since when?"

She cocked her head to the side. "After the talk shows but before the evening news?"

I laughed. The girl told time by what was on TV. She was ridiculous.

It was fucking adorable.

She tilted her head and pointed at the bags.

"What's that?"

"I got you some stuff. Actually, hold on."

I went back outside and shook my head. I must be a sucker. Hell, there was no doubt about it at this point.

My peaceful cabin was about to be invaded and it was all for her.

I opened the back door and the dog jumped out, wagging his entire body in joy. I grabbed his leash and the cat carrier that I'd somehow gotten two enormous cats into.

They'd been surprisingly well-behaved for me. Thank goodness. I hadn't been in the mood to wrestle.

Well, maybe with her…

I had no idea how to take care of these animals. But I'd promised her and Mason. It was part of the deal.

And I couldn't wait to see her face when I brought them inside. Maybe she'd smile at me again. The girl could light up a room with that megawatt smile.

As soon as I got inside, I knew it was worth it. She didn't squeal like a girl. She just froze, one hand holding up a pair of bright pink panties. Then she smiled at me, a real smile.

Her whole face lit up. It knocked my damn socks off. My God the girl was beautiful.

"I brought you some friends."

"Oh, I see. Thank you. And also… panties?"

I would have laughed but the sight of her holding those sexy things up made me freeze in place. I wanted to see those things on her. So I could tear them off.

With my teeth.

I cleared my throat.

"You only packed two pairs. I figured you might need more stuff while we sort everything out. Easier than doing laundry every other day."

I set the cat case down and let the creatures out. I hoped they didn't destroy everything in house or piss everywhere. I'd got them food and a new litter box too.

I'd been a busy boy. Running errands for her. I was fucking whipped and I hadn't even gotten a taste.

I wanted to see some real appreciation dammit.

"There's other stuff too." I stared at her. "Not just..."

"Panties."

She nodded, finishing my sentence. She seemed to realize she was holding them in the air because she dropped them into the bag. She gracefully bent her knee to call the animals over to her.

They surrounded her, rubbing against her for attention as she knelt on the floor. I was a dirty old man, no doubt about it.

Because all I could think was- *damn, she looks good on her knees.*

"Thank you Connor. Thank you so much."

She stared up at me, her eyes sweet and soft and sincere. There was that appreciation I was looking for. There was just one little problem.

How the hell was I going to turn it into what I really wanted?

CASSANDRA

"That's a good boy. That's a good boy!"

I sounded like an idiot. But Besos was licking my face and I could not have been happier.

Well, if I hadn't witnessed a murder and put my only friend in the world in mortal danger.

But right now, Connor said Mase was safe. I was safe and the fuzzy ones were safe. And I was buzzed as fuck.

"Did you eat?"

"Uh huh."

Connor was staring at me as I sat on the floor getting my face licked. He looked like he wasn't sure if he wanted to laugh or throw up.

"That's not sanitary."

"Probably not."

"The alcohol might take care of the germs."

"Maybe."

I was laughing as I tried to push Besos away. Connor took pity on me and pulled his leash away. Then he got busy in the kitchen, setting up bowls and a litter pan in the bathroom down the hall.

I reached into the shopping bags again and stared at a bright blue top. I pulled out an orange shirt and camo patterned leggings.

"Why is everything so bright? Are we going hunting or something?"

He glanced over his shoulder at me, looking sheepish.

"So you don't get lost."

"Lost?"

He grinned.

"In the woods."

I scowled, pretending to be mad. It was high-handed and bossy and weirdly controlling of him to buy me clothes.

But I couldn't be mad. It was kind of sweet. Plus, after seeing those pictures- that he'd lost his partner-his best friend- I saw him differently.

Connor had a heart. He could be hurt. He wasn't just a mindless, ridiculously hot FBI drone sent to annoy me. He was human now. Human and somehow, not so out of reach.

Not so different from me or Mase. We'd all had our hearts crushed and picked up the pieces. We were all just doing our damned best.

He just happened to look insanely handsome doing it.

I grinned at him, deciding to make nice. He'd bought me stuff. I was in a good mood, why not spread it around?

"What are we doing now?"

He sat down and reached for the bottle. My eyes got wide as he poured himself a man-sized shot.

"We could talk."

I shook my head. I knew he'd just ask a thousand questions I couldn't answer. I saw his eyes land on the poker chips and light up.

"Or… we could play."

I smiled at him.

"Oh, you are so on."

CONNOR

"**H**ere, have a lemon."

I watched her tip her head back, taking the shot. She'd insisted on the salt, so I'd done the gentlemanly thing and got her some lemon slices and a beer chaser.

Lick it. Slam it. Suck it.

Three things I would love to be doing right now.

To her.

"This is aiding and abetting underage drinking, isn't it?"

I smiled. Yes, it most definitely was. I was willfully intoxicating an underage drinker. True, she was close to twenty-one. According to her ID anyway, which I suspected was fake. But it was still wrong.

And I had ulterior motives for doing it.

To get her to talk of course.

That's what I told myself anyway. It had nothing to do with the way she looked sitting there, all free and giggly and young. She was so fresh and pretty, it took my breath away.

I sat back and stared at her. She was glowing. Sparkling somehow. Her attitude towards me had clearly done a one eighty.

And all I'd done was bring her pets.

Of course, the tequila might be playing a role too.

I loosened the collar of my shirt and took a long sip of my beer. If I was going to be a bastard, I was going to be a *fucking bastard.*

And I wanted to be buzzed for it.

"Do you play poker?"

She nodded and I smiled inwardly. The little snoop had given me a brilliant idea.

I carried the box of chips over and set it down. She reached out and ran her fingers over it. I brushed my hand over hers and opened the box. Our eyes met and a shock ran up my arm.

And that was just from her fingers.

I cleared my throat and pulled out a deck of cards.

"Should I deal?"

She arched a brow.

"What are we playing for?"

I smiled, having a brilliant idea. I could kill two birds with one stone. Further my investigation. And get a peak at Casey's gorgeous body.

"An answer. Or a piece of clothing."

She laughed and sipped her beer.

"You mean like truth or strip?" I nodded and she tilted her head, considering. "What do you want to know?"

"Nothing too crazy. I'm just curious about you. Call it a hazard of the job."

She set her beer down and rested her elbows on her knees. Her eyes were twinkling as she heaved an exaggerated sigh.

"Okayyyyy fine. But I can ask for whatever I want."

I nodded, conceding.

"Within reason."

"Fine."

"Fine."

She giggled and hiccuped. I laughed at her. A genuine, deep, belly laugh. It had been years since I'd spontaneously laughed like that.

She was toast. I finally had her where I wanted her. The girl was putty in my hands. I'd thrown in the strip part to throw her off the scent.

Also because I felt like I would explode if I didn't get her clothes off.

"First bets."

She lifted her leg and wiggled her bare toes at me. The chain jangled. I knew what she was going to say before she opened her luscious mouth.

"If I win, I want this off." She grinned. "And then I want a foot rub."

I stared at her cute little foot, imagining it in my lap. Hmmm... her pink painted toes looked tasty. I'd never been into feet before, but I could probably develop a fetish where this girl was concerned.

I nodded and started to deal, deciding to throw the first round.

Oh yeah, this was a win/win.

CASSANDRA

"Hmmm, a little to the left."

Connor's huge hands enveloped my foot. My newly freed foot. I sipped my beer. It tasted even better now that I had my freedom.

Temporarily anyway.

I'd won the first two hands easily and he'd unchained me without too much grumbling.

Now, he was giving me a world-class foot massage. I would never have imagined for a moment that the agent was such an excellent masseuse.

But he was. Oh my goodness, he was.

His rough fingertips kneaded the arch of my foot. I practically purred as he paused to deal another hand. Then he casually went back to stroking the underside of my foot with one hand and holding his cards with the other.

Hmmm… heaven…

I squirmed a bit, feeling strangely restless. It was getting warm in here, though that probably had something to do with the view.

Connor was naked from the waist up.

I'd asked for his shirt on the second round and he'd asked for mine. Thankfully, he was the one who'd had to strip. I smiled at him and looked at my cards. A pair of tens. Ha! He'd be in his boxer shorts in no time.

I snuck another look at his chest. He was… really well put together. It was hard not to notice how thick his arms and shoulders were too.

How solid and wide and- well, manly.

I was not going to stare at his stomach though. That was just rude. He didn't seem to notice where I was looking anyway. He was too busy staring at his cards.

He'd lost the first two hands and he *did not* look happy about it. But he was being a good sport. I wondered how long he'd rub my foot and decided not to ask.

I'd never gotten a foot rub before. Well, other than at the pedi place. This was different though.

This was better.

"Bet?"

"If I win, I get to do whatever I want with this."

He ran the edge of his finger up the bottom of my foot and I inhaled. Somehow, that finger of his felt like it was touching me somewhere else.

Somewhere private.

"Are you going to eat it?"

He smiled and poured us each another shot. I'd been afraid he was going to ask me about the case. But so far on each hand he just kept trying to get me to take my top off.

I giggled, realizing Mason was right.

Connor did have a crush on me.

"Where is Mase?"

"Is that your prize? You want to know where he is?"

I sobered instantly.

"I just want to know if he's okay."

He rubbed his fingers into my heel and I felt myself relax.

"He's okay. I promise."

"You aren't going to tell me where he is are you?"

"Nope. Pick something else."

I grinned and picked up my shot.

"I think you would be more comfortable-" We clinked our shot glass together. "Without pants."

He choked on his shot, but I swallowed mine down with barely a wince. I was getting the hang of this drinking thing. I liked it. I felt like was good at it.

Casey Jones, she had a knack for three things: landing in trouble, shaking her bootie, and getting hammered!

I picked my cards up again and he asked me if I wanted to swap any out. I held up two fingers. I grinned as I looked at my new hand, realizing I now had two pairs.

His face was hard and strained. I had a feeling I had won. I was going to see the guy in his boxer shorts in a hot minute. It might be crazy, and reckless, and very risky, but I wanted to see those shorts dammit.

I was grinning ear to ear as I wondered what color they were.

After that he would *have* to answer my questions. He had nowhere to go from there. I highly doubted he would sit there completely naked.

I smiled to myself. There was no reason not to enjoy the view. He was a very good-looking man. There was no arguing with that.

Just because we were on opposite sides of the law-

"Call."

"Two pairs. Read them and weep."

He just smiled at me.

My eyes got wide as he laid his cards down. The bastard had a full house. He squeezed my foot and leaned back.

"Hmmmm… this little piggy went to market…"

"What are you-"

"Shhhh…"

He grabbed the salt and the lemon wedges and pulled them across the table to him. He lifted my foot and looked at it.

Then he smiled and licked it.

Slowly, he ran his hot, wet tongue up top of my foot from my ankle all the way to my toes. I gasped at the feel of his tongue on my skin. He shook salt over the spot and smiled. Then he held a lemon wedge and put it between two of my toes.

"Squeeze."

I pinched my toes together and exhaled shakily as he poured a shot. I knew what he was doing. He was doing a body shot off my damn foot.

And it was giving me all kinds of crazy feelings.

He grinned and licked the salt off my foot. Slowly and thoroughly. Then he did the shot. What he did next made me slide a little lower in my seat.

He sucked the lemon. And my toes. Oh lord, he wasn't in a hurry about it either. I moaned and he opened his eyes. That's when I felt his tongue swirl over my toes and between them. He stroked the sensitive spot between two of my middle toes and I felt it between my legs.

He knew it too. He looked at me *right freaking there* while he worked his tongue in and out of the little space between my toes. There was no mistaking it. He stared at my pussy as his tongue slid in and out as I slowly turned to mush.

"Oh…"

He lowered my foot to his lap and winked at me.

"Next hand, I want that shirt."

CONNOR

"So. Where did you grow up?"

She frowned, adjusting that tiny little scrap of stretchy lace she called a camisole. It was cropped and barely covered her ribs. I stared at the silky roundness of her breasts, letting my eyes sink lower to the soft curve of her taut belly.

I could do a shot out of that belly button. I'd lick up every drop. Hmmm... maybe later.

"That's a complicated question."

I'd won two hands in a row now. She was topless, more or less, and I still had that sexy little foot of hers in my lap. I was rubbing her leg now, my fingers sliding up and under the edge of her jeans.

They were just stretchy enough for my fingers to graze the back of her knee. Every time I did it, she lost her train of thought. I smiled to myself.

Casey Jones had very sensitive skin.

Silky, and smooth and warm and so tender I wanted to lick every inch of it. I thought she might let me. Hell, if I kept teasing her like this, she might even beg me.

I would have given every damn thing I owned to hear her beg.

But not tonight. I was not an animal. I would control myself tonight. I groaned as her foot brushed my cock. I knew she didn't mean to do it but it nearly snapped my last thread of control.

The fact that she wanted me too… well that was only making it harder. The girl was clearly inexperienced and not good at hiding her response to me. And damn if I didn't like that about her.

Still, it didn't seem right to take advantage of the situation.

She was drunk and horny and might well be a virgin. I grinned to myself as I noticed how hard her nipples were. I might be taking the moral high ground but I sure did like making her horny.

If I was going to be pent up and frustrated, well then, so was she.

"I have all night. Pay up, Jones."

I pulled my fingers away, dragging them down her gracefully curved calf. Her skin was so juicy and plump. I felt like a big, bad wolf, thinking about eating a lamb.

And what a sweet little lamb she was.

Her eyes lifted to mine and I froze at the raw honesty reflected there. Raw and painful. She exhaled shakily.

"You know that's not my real name."

I nodded slowly, putting the deck of cards aside. I had been about to deal again, or try to with one hand. But she deserved my full attention.

Both hands slid to her leg, making comforting circles. No teasing now. I wanted to soothe her.

I wanted to *know*.

She looked away and shrugged.

"I was born near Charlotte. I had a nice family. Not rich, but nice."

Had. She said 'had.' I felt my stomach clench up.

And then I realized that was all she was going to say.

"How did they die?"

Her eyes shot to mine and I regretted the question immediately.

"Sorry."

She shook her head.

"It's okay. It was a long time ago."

I felt something inside me crack open. She was so real. There was no artifice in her. She was so strong to have survived everything she'd been through.

And yet in that moment, she looked like a broken-hearted little girl.

"How did you end up with Mason?"

She raised an eyebrow at me, looking playful again. But I could tell she was putting on a brave face.

"Is that your stake?"

I shook my head slowly. I wanted her jeans off. It was stupid and dangerous and wrong. But I was battling with the inner caveman inside me.

And I was losing.

"No. I want these."

I tugged on her jeans and she blushed.

"Fine. We play for pants."

I smiled slowly and picked the cards up.

"Pants it is."

CASSANDRA

He'd taken my damn pants.

I tugged my knees up and then put them back down again as he smiled at his cards. His smile widened as I tried to find a way to arrange my legs that was somewhat ladylike.

I'd caught him looking me over twice already. Even now he was peeking at my legs over the top of his cards. I could practically *feel* them as they slid up and down my thighs.

He wasn't even trying to hide it! He hadn't stared between my legs but I knew the cotton of my panties was thin.

I knew he could see more than he should!

And he still had his damn pants.

He raised a lazy eyebrow and the smile dropped as he looked at my face. My face! Instead of my body.

"Stakes?"

I grit my teeth.

"Pants!"

He shook his head.

"You really are a glutton for punishment."

I crossed my arms.

"What do you want?"

He grinned at me and this time he did look between my legs. I gasped as his eyes flitted up to my breasts next, like he was considering... dammit, there was no way I was going to get actually naked!

He sighed and shook his head. He opened his mouth, as if he was going to speak and sighed again.

"Don't you dare!"

His eyes snapped to mine and I braced myself.

"I want to know about Dante."

"What about him?"

He smiled.

"Everything."

I lifted my chin. I wasn't going to tell him about the murder no matter what. But I could tell him other stuff.

"You'll have to win the hand first."

He tossed his cards down and leaned back, his hand on his waist band. I'd noticed his bulge before but now it was different.

It was… bulgier.

The man looked like that part of him was oversized too. Like his damn ego! I bristled as he grinned at me.

"So. Dante."

He waited, his eyes on my body. He started at my feet and travelled up. I shrugged, crossing my arms over my chest.

"He comes in."

"Yeah?"

His eyes were on my face now. On my lips.

"He… likes me."

Now he was looking at me. Paying attention. He looked disturbed.

"I stay away from him as much as I can. I know if he and Mason got into a fight, he'd do something nuts. He scares the shit out of me."

"He should."

I swallowed and reached for the cards.

"Stakes?"

"That's it?"

I nodded stubbornly. He exhaled and shook his head at me.

"That wasn't really enough to satisfy me, honey."

"Fine. Name your prize."

He smiled slowly, his eyes on my panties again.

"Don't even think about it!"

He shook his head slowly, like he was disappointed. Then he stood up and grabbed his jacket. I stared as he pulled my battered old romance novel out and held it up.

"How about a bed time story?"

"What?"

"How about a bedtime story instead? I think we've had enough cards for the night."

Considering I had almost hardly any clothes left to lose, it wasn't a bad idea. I yawned and nodded. He was being strangely magnanimous. I knew he'd expected me to tell him more about Dante.

"Okay."

"I want a reenactment."

"A what?"

He smiled and held the book up.

"I read. You reenact."

I swallowed and stared at him. That book was... dirty. It was about a master and a sub. It was about stuff I knew nothing about, not really.

Even if I had read the damn book a bunch of times.

I stared at him as he flipped through and started reading.

CONNOR

"Jasmine assumed the position."

I cleared my throat. Casey was staring at me, bright red on her pretty cheeks. She looked outraged.

She also looked curious. More than a little bit. She hadn't told me to go to hell.

Not yet anyway.

What the fuck are you doing, Conn? Just fuck her already. That's what you want to do. Fuck her so hard the walls come crashing down around you.

I shook my head as if to clear it. Shut up Danny. You are not helping.

Stop playing games. You're going to lose your job over this anyway. Maybe more. Because Mason is going to fucking kill you. You might as well get a taste of her- just a taste-

Danny was right. I might as well-

No. No no no.

I cleared my throat again.

"Jasmine knelt in front of her master, her back straight and her eyes demurely lowered."

I rested the book on my lap and looked at Casey expectantly. Like I knew what I was doing. Like I wasn't playing with fucking fire.

"I'm waiting."

"You want me to- to kneel?"

She looked so uncertain. I smiled at her, my eyes on her collarbone. Skin shouldn't look so touchable. The girl practically glowed.

"It's your book."

"It's my friends- Daphne. She loaned it to me-"

I shook my head.

"You don't have any friends. Now, unless you want to take off another piece of clothing..."

She exhaled shakily and I felt like a bastard. For exactly two seconds. Because after those two seconds she walked over to me and started lowering herself to her knees.

Oh my fucking Christ.

"Closer."

Her eyes darted up and she swallowed. Then she moved in. Right between my thighs.

Her eyes were on the floor as she knelt there, waiting.

I picked up the book again, my heart pulsing all the blood in my body to my engorged cock. I was doing this to myself.

"Her lips were open and waiting for her master's touch. Her thighs sweetly parted."

I skimmed ahead. Jesus, who wrote this shit? It was fucking filthy. I wasn't going to be able to read much more without crossing the line.

All the lines.

"She put her head on her master's thigh and begged him to allow her to pleasure him. With a groan he agreed."

My mouth was dry as Casey hesitated and rested her cheek on my thigh. She didn't beg though. She didn't have to.

I could have had her right then and there. On the floor. On the chair. I closed the book, my voice low and rough.

"She had been a good girl. His pleasure was her reward."

My hand reached out and stroked her hair away from her face. Her eyes were closed. She was trembling slightly. I groaned as I realized her lips were open. Her thighs too.

Just like in the book.

I scooped her up and held her in my arms. For a heartbeat, I just stared at her, so ready to carry her up the stairs to my bed.

Instead I lowered her to the couch and leaned over her, my lips hovering just above hers.

Her breath came in little gasps, like a tiny bunny. I was struggling to control myself. To stop myself from doing something bad.

Something bad that would feel way too good.

We stared into each other's eyes, neither of us moving.

Well, I was moving. Just one hand. Reaching... lower... wrapping my fingers around the silky leg of her calf...

Her eyes widened as I snapped the cuff back into place.

CASSANDRA

'**E**AT ME.'

I stared at the note propped up on the coffee table. It leaned against a bagel. I could smell coffee brewing in the kitchen.

It must have been set on a timer, because I was alone.

I lifted the blanket and looked down at myself.

Mostly naked and alone.

I groaned and grabbed my head. It was throbbing. My mouth was dry and felt fuzzy. *What the hell had happened last night?* I was not ready to eat a bagel, but I did notice more writing on the back.

I picked up the note and flipped it over.

'*OJ in the fridge. Drink it all.*'

I forced myself to stand and padded barefoot over to the kitchen.

I noticed the pets had been fed and watered. Good. Because if I had to bend over I had a feeling I would upchuck all over the nice hardwood floor.

I swung open the fridge. A bottle of OJ sat there with a smiley face post-it note stuck to it. I wanted to punch that smiley face.

Instead, I pulled out the OJ and poured a glass. I leaned against the kitchen island and drank half of it. Then I filled the glass again and shuffled back to the couch.

The sound of the chain clanging against the floor reminded me that Connor was a bastard. He had left me here alone and hungover. Chained up like a dog.

Still, he *had* fed me.

I sat down and forced myself to eat a bite of the bagel. I chewed slowly and took another bite. I thought about turning the TV on and decided it would hurt my head too much.

I wondered where Mason was and if he was mad at me. I wondered where Conn was and why he was such a bastard. I wondered why I had been naked when I woke up.

I wondered why I wasn't more concerned about that.

PING.

I glanced down. There was a text on that locked phone of his. I put the bagel down and picked up the phone.

You alive?

Barely.

I could almost hear him laugh. I wanted to talk though. I had a few really weird memories that were all a blur.

Any news? How's Mason?

He's safe. That's all I can say ATM.

What happened last night?

You don't remember? I'm offended.

Dude, I am not wearing clothes. Did we... do anything?

Sweetheart, I promise you that you would know if we had.

I chewed my lip, staring at the phone. He was being daft. Or deliberately obtuse. I decided to keep pushing. Besides, texting with Connor was strangely fun.

But... why am I naked?

You were not naked when I left.

Okay, almost naked.

Oh that...

Yes. That.

You really shouldn't drink so much. We played strip poker. You were losing.

Oh. So I was naked and you were a gentleman.

I didn't say I was a gentleman. But I would not take you the first time when you were black out drunk.

I stared at the phone.

Take me. He said take me. Images of his huge hands lifting me up and throwing me over his shoulder came to mind.

PING.

The phone beeped again and I realized I was gripping it so hard my fingers were turning white. I'd been trying to think of something witty to say, with zero luck.

No matter how tempting it was.

Oh. My. God.

My breath was shaky as I stared at the phone. I set it down and scooted away from it. Like it was a snake and I was afraid it would bite me.

But I wanted it to bite me. I was hungover and confused and trapped and worried. But that didn't change a thing about the heat building low in my belly.

All I could think about was what he had just said. That he had been tempted.

And how badly I wanted him to give in.

I realized my headache was fading and finished the bagel. I put the volume on low as I flipped through my favorite channels. I drank two more glasses of orange juice before I fell asleep with Cheeto on my lap.

CONNOR

"You are free to go."

"Like fucking hell I am."

"Mase, if you won't talk, it's going to have to be her."

"I didn't see anything. And she didn't see anything! She would have said something to me dammit!"

"Trust me, Mase. She did."

"Don't fucking call me that. Only she calls me that."

Mason ran his hands through his hair. He sat down heavily. I crossed my arms, waiting for the inevitable to sink in.

"You're sure?"

"I'm sure. She's scared out of her mind. Mostly about you."

"Promise me one thing, DeWitt."

"If I can."

"You won't hurt her."

I nodded slowly. The last thing I wanted to do was hurt the beautiful girl. That's why I had hidden her away and risked my job.

I wanted to protect her. I needed to. Among the many other things I wanted to do with her. Less noble things.

Filthy, dirty things.

But there was no reason to tell Mason that. Besides, he already knew I wanted her. He just had no idea how bad.

There was a sharp knock at the door. Micky's face appeared in the window. I went out into the hallway to talk to him. He handed me a plastic box with Mason's personal effects.

"The prints on the bloody roses vase came in. We got a match."

"Let me guess. It's dead Hell Raiser number two."

"Yeah, how did you-"

"Never mind. Check his clothes and bike to see if he's a match for the fibers on the first body."

"You got it. Oh, and Conn?"

"Yeah?"

"Nobody has seen the waitress lately. The pretty little one from The Jar. Any idea?"

I stared at him.

"Who is asking?"

"Sheil wanted to bring her in again for another interview. She thought maybe she'd do better being questioned by a woman."

"I don't think it will go anywhere."

163

"Why not?"

"She didn't see anything. I told the girl to keep a low profile. Obviously, she listened to me. I'll talk to Sheil."

"Thanks man."

And just like that, I had broken the code. Lied to one of my own. Casey was worth it though. It's not like she was the key to bringing down the gang that had killed my partner or anything.

Unless she was.

Fuck me. I closed my eyes and tried to get my shit together. I was an idiot and my dick was getting in the way. All I could think about was her and it was interfering with solving this case.

So, only one thing left to do.

Let the beast out of it's cage. Feed it what it wanted. Then maybe I could fucking focus again. Put this insane infatuation aside and be objective about all of this.

About her.

I went back into the interrogation room and tossed Mason his stuff.

"We're letting you go. But I'm putting guys on you."

"What the fuck, DeWitt!"

"I promised her."

He cursed and stormed out. I debated about giving him a ride and decided against it. He might try and choke me.

Besides, I wanted to get home.

I needed to see her. My body hadn't stopped aching for her since last night. I knew I'd done the right thing when I put the breaks on before kissing her.

No matter how hard that had been.

She was a witness. She was too young. She knew something and she was lying about it. I knew it might all lead me to Danny's killer.

But I didn't care anymore. I would solve the crime and make his killer pay. Danny would understand it if I took a little detour.

Tonight, I was taking what was mine.

CASSANDRA

I turned the hot water on again, for the third time.

Oh yes, this is just what the doctor ordered. A bagel, juice, a nap and a hot bath. I let my arm dangle over the edge of the tub and sighed.

Besos sat on the floor, staring at the chain as it dripped water onto the floor. Cheeto was passed out underneath the radiator. Even Morely was sitting on the toilet staring at me.

Me and my shackle were taking a bath. A very long bath. In fact, I wasn't sure I ever wanted to get out again.

I only wished I had a book.

A book.

I sat up in the tub, the memories of last night crashing in on me.

I had- we had- he had read from my book! And- I blinked. That was it. Nothing had *actually* happened. But I had kneeled.

Kneeled!

Ugh! That bastard had not been nearly as drunk as I had been! Oh God, he'd licked my toes too!

I squeezed my thighs together at the memory. His touch on my skin… his lips and tongue against my sensitive toes. The truth was, I had wanted him to do way more than lick my toes.

Much, much more.

I leaned back in the tub and stared at the ceiling. I'd been half-naked and willing. He'd been practically drooling as he looked me over. The man had looked at me like he wanted to eat me for dinner. And shameful or not, I would have let him.

But he hadn't.

Shit, maybe he was a gentleman after all.

I heard a car pull up. The door to the bathroom was not shut because of the chain. I sunk a little lower under the bubbles, realizing I was about to be *for real* naked in front of him.

Ugh, the stupid foam was fading fast.

That's what happens when you use shower gel as bubble bath, Cass.

I heard the door open and footsteps cross the room. I frantically swirled my hands to make the bubbles get bubblier.

It didn't work. In fact, it was having the opposite effect. My body was clearly visible beneath the surface of the water.

Shit shit shit!

The door opened slowly. I crossed my arms over my chest and pulled my knees up.

"Excuse me!"

He leaned against the doorframe and crossed his arms. He didn't smile or apologize. And he made no move to leave either!

"How long have you been in there?"

I shrugged.

"Are you clean yet?"

I scowled at him, indignant at the implication that I had not been clean before.

"Yes!"

"Are you drunk?"

"Ugh! No!"

"Good."

He stared at me, not smiling. He looked so intense. Then he knelt and reached into the tub.

He lifted his hand and held up the drain stopper. The water swirled around me as it started to empty out.

He held out his hand. I stared at it. If I took his hand, I had to let go of my boob. If I let go of my boob, the jig was up. I'd be a willing participant in flashing him.

But maybe that wasn't such a bad thing.

"Casey."

168

I shut my eyes. This was not happening. I had just been imagining him touching me and now I was naked in front of him!

And he looked pissed! Was it because I used half his shower gel? Not exactly the fantasy I had in mind!

"Stand up."

I shook my head and he sighed. The next thing I knew I was wrapped in a towel and being lifted up and into his arms. He headed for the stairs. The chain brought us up short.

He cursed and stopped, unchaining my ankle. Then he looked at my foot. The toes were kinda wrinkly.

"How long were you in there anyway?"

"A- a while."

He shook his head at me and carried me up the stairs. He stopped at the doorway at the front of the house and kicked it open. I'd never seen this room before but I knew instantly that it was his.

There was a bed and a dresser with a chair by the window. That was it. But it was warm and inviting just the same. It was spare and masculine and just... his.

"What are you doing?"

He lowered me to the bed and started pulling his clothes off.

"What do you think I'm doing?"

I stared at him.

"You are… changing your clothes?"

His shirt was already unbuttoned, revealing his hard, smooth chest. He shrugged it off and reached for his shoes. They hit the floor one at a time.

"No."

He reached for his pants. I watched in fascination as he unbuttoned them and started sliding them over his hips.

"Admitting you cheated at poker last night and paying up out of guilt?"

He stood there in his boxer briefs. His hand pressed down on his dick, clearly outlined through the gray cotton. His enormous dick.

His big, huge, very hard dick.

My mouth dropped open.

"No."

"Huh?"

I looked at his face. He was smiling at me faintly. I realized we had been having a conversation. He'd distracted me with the monster in his shorts.

He crossed to the foot of the bed and pulled me up to stand in front of him. He brushed my hair back and gripped the edge of the towel.

"How are you feeling?"

"Okay."

"Hangover gone?"

"Yes."

"Good."

Then he lifted his hand and slowly pulled the towel away. His eyes flared as he looked down at my body. But only for a second. Because he was on me, pulling me against him, his hot mouth colliding with mine.

My damp breasts smashed against his hot, smooth chest. I moaned as my hands found his thick shoulders. His hands were in my hair, tangling it as he moved my head, tilting it and guiding my jaw down so he could get his tongue inside.

I whimpered as his hands slid lower, holding my back so that I was flush against him. His narrow hips pressed into mine. I felt the heat of him- the power and strength of his throbbing cock as it pressed against me insistently.

I could barely think. But there was one thought that kept circling.

Connor was finally kissing me. This was my first kiss. Connor was my first kiss.

And as far as first kisses went, this one was pretty much taking no prisoners.

"Hmm... Jesus, Casey... lay down for me sweetheart."

I didn't say a word. Didn't have to. Because he lifted me and then I was on my back. Connor held himself above me, kissing me as his hands started to wander.

He leaned down and kissed my breasts one at a time. Then my lips. Then my breasts again.

"God, you are perfect. How can you be so perfect?"

He pulled me up towards him as he rocked against me, his cock circling on my belly. He wasn't going slow. This was the sexual equivalent of being thrown in the deep end of the pool on your first day at swim class.

I was naked. He was almost naked. This was happening. After all these years, 'it' was finally happening. I arched against him and said his name as his fingers slid between my legs.

I whimpered as he toyed with my folds, slowly sliding a finger inside me. I cried out as he worked his thick finger in and out of my body.

"Oh God, sweetheart. You're so tight…"

He lowered his head, kissing his way down my body. I felt his tongue slide over my pussy lips and moaned. Then he pulled my clit into his mouth and flicked his tongue against it.

I screamed.

He didn't stop the rapid pulse of his tongue on my most sensitive spot. He held me down as my entire body bounced on the bed. I was coming, as the saying goes, and much harder than I ever had on my own.

He murmured words of encouragement and then I felt it. A second finger was pushing inside me, opening me up.

I whimpered in pain and he froze, staring up at me. He'd draped my thighs over his shoulders. I blushed at how intimate it was. How hot he looked, his eyes glazed with lust for me.

Connor DeWitt was officially chowing down on my box. And the man was in it to win it. He wasn't shy about it. He was just... having at me.

Like I was a giant steak and he hadn't eaten in a week.

"Sweetheart?"

"Ah- yes?"

"Fuck. Is this- has anyone done this to you before?"

"No."

"No to which part?"

"No to... any of it."

He cursed and rolled away. He covered his eyes with his arm, breathing heavily.

"Fuck. Fuck fuck fuck."

I rolled towards him and laid a hand on his chest. He flinched and slowly took my hand, moving it away and setting in on the bed beside him.

"Careful Case. I'm barely holding on. You should- *oh God I cant believe I'm saying this-* you should put some clothes on."

"Why?"

"Because I'm going to hurt you. I won't mean to. But you are so small and I am- I need to take a cold shower or something."

I snuggled up to him, laying my chin on his shoulder. I slid my leg up along his and he groaned like he was in agony.

"I don't want to put my clothes on. I don't want you to stop."

He moaned and I watched in fascination as his cock actually moved up and down in his briefs. All by itself. I reached out to touch it and he caught my wrist.

"Casey-"

"You were my first kiss."

He held perfectly still except his hand slid against mine, rubbing my palm.

"I was?"

"Yes."

He cursed and his cock flexed again. This time he didn't stop me when I reached out to trace it through his shorts.

"Don't you want me to be my first everything?"

"Yes. Fuck yes."

"Why don't you finish what you started?"

He moaned and turned to stare at me.

"Sweetheart, I'm not going to be able to go slow-you deserve-"

I pressed a kiss to his stomach and he hissed the air out of his lungs.

"I deserve what?"

"Someone who can control themselves, not a wild fucking animal."

"I like animals."

That was it. I gasped as the bed shook. If I had even blinked I might have missed it. I might have missed him literally pouncing on my body. He was tugging his shorts down as he threw my legs apart.

Then I felt him against me. There. His bare cock was sliding up and down against me. It felt good.

SO good.

"I can't stop now sweetheart. I'm sorry."

He grunted as the tip of his cock slipped inside me.

"Ohhh…"

He kissed me passionately, his tongue stroking mine as he sunk a little further in.

"Open for me sweetheart… try to relax… Jesus Christ, it's too much. It shouldn't feel this good."

I felt my body clench on him and he moaned like a man who was being tortured. His chest skimmed my nipples as he flinched away from me.

"Did I hurt you?"

He laughed but it sounded strained. He cupped my cheek and pressed a soft kiss against my lips.

"No sweetheart. You might kill me with pleasure though. I want to- fuck! I want to move."

"Move?"

"Yes. Oh my fucking God you are so tight... I want to-"

I circled my hips against him experimentally.

"Like this?"

He squeezed his eyes shut like he was in pain again. I *was* hurting him.

"Conn-"

"Shhhh... it's okay. I'm fine. I just. Let me try to do this nice and slow."

"Okay... but I want to move too."

He cursed and pulled out slightly. Then he came back in and we both moaned. He kissed me and did it again. And again.

Each time he seemed to get a little further inside me.

"So sweet. So tight."

His hands gripped my hips and he pushed a little harder. I gasped as I was stretched open on his shaft. He was… thicker than I was.

By a lot.

"Conn?"

His hips were moving faster now- and he wasn't being as gentle. It hurt a little. And then he withdrew and pushed into me. Hard.

"Ow!"

"Oh God… I'm sorry Case, I can't stop. It's too late- fuck- uhhh- nothing could make me stop-"

He held my hips down as he worked his cock in and out of me, going all the way in with each stroke. The pain was starting to subside. There was so much pressure. I was so stretched open for him. I felt like I was reaching for something, just out of reach.

He leaned back without stopping the relentless motion of his cock. In and out. In and out. Hard and fast. I could hear his ragged breathing as he kissed my neck and then lower. He licked the line of my cleavage, pulling a nipple into his mouth and sucking.

I arched off the bed as my body shattered into a million pieces of light.

"Oh! Oh! Oh!"

"That's it sweetheart- unf- milk me- you-"

He groaned and started pumping his hips wildly. I held onto his massive shoulders as he rode me hard and fast, his balls slapping my skin with each fierce thrust.

I was still shaking from the force of his orgasm as I felt him expand inside me. Something was about to happen. Something big.

Then he roared.

My body squeezed him, holding on tight as his cock pulsed deep inside me. I felt a wet, delicious warmth fill me up.

And then I realized what it was.

"Conn."

He kissed me, his gorgeous face damp with sweat. He was shaking as he held his hips flush against mine, his cock jerking inside me as he finished.

"Sweetheart... oh God... so good..."

He moaned and I felt his cock twitch inside me. I was shivering with aftershocks from my orgasm. But I was also more than a little worried as I realized something. What we had skipped.

"Shouldn't we have used a condom?"

CONNOR

"This isn't a one-night stand. We don't need condoms."

I don't know what made me say that, but the moment I did, I knew I meant it. I was keeping her.

Not that there had really been any doubt about that. I mean, the girl had been chained up in my living room. I'd been kidding myself when I said I would get her out of my system. It wasn't possible.

I knew now without a doubt that I was never letting her go.

But putting it into words... well, that was a whole other story. And yeah, I hadn't really thought the whole no condom thing through either.

I was too out of my mind with animal lust to do that.

I still was. In fact... the beauty beneath me stared up at me. My balls seemed to get heavy and full in seconds. I felt my cock rising to the occasion again. After what, ten seconds?

That had to be some sort of record.

"We don't?"

"No. We don't."

I shook my head. I didn't expand on why we didn't need a condom. We didn't need one because I wanted her knocked up. The caveman inside me wanted to own her in every sense of the word.

I knew I was taking advantage of her innocence. But at the moment, I didn't much care.

I kissed her hard, letting my hands wander down to her hips again. I didn't feel like talking. My cock was enveloped in the sweetest place on Earth. Her body felt like living silk, undulating around me as I started to harden.

Started? Hell, I was already at full capacity. But this was a whole new level of erect. My cock was so hard it could have cut glass.

And we were just getting started.

It was going to be a long night. I hoped to God that she could keep up. But fuck, she was so small. I might have hurt her...

"Are you sore?"

"What? You mean-"

I kissed her as she trailed off, clearly embarrassed. My cock was inside her, and so was my come. It was a little late to be shy.

But it was still pretty fucking adorable.

"Yes. I mean *that.*"

"Oh." She blushed and wiggled a little bit beneath me. "No. I'm fine."

I said a brief prayer of thanks to the Heavenly Father.

"That's good, sweetheart. That's real good."

I smiled and grabbed one of her thighs, wrapping it around my waist.

She looked surprised as hell as I started to move again. I groaned as I slid in and out of her heat. It was easier to move now. She'd been so tight before. But I'd unleashed a huge load inside her already.

Oh yeah, this was going to get messy.

"You feel so amazing, sweetheart…"

Her eyes closed as I worked my cock in and out of her, going as deep as I could with each stroke. Our chests rubbed, her nipples teasing my skin as I slid against her.

Hmmfff… sex wasn't supposed to feel this good. It never had for me. Not even close. It wasn't in the same ballpark.

Hell, it wasn't even the same sport.

It was like before her I'd been walking around wrapped in cellophane. Or bubble wrap. My senses were numbed. But with her… all my senses were alive.

Every single nerve in my body was awake and jumping for fucking joy.

Especially my cock. Dear Jesus, my cock was in actual heaven. And Casey was whimpering softly, enjoying it as much as I was.

But if I wasn't careful, I was going to pop. And I wasn't ready for this to be over.

"Hold on, sweetheart. I have to-"

I groaned and flipped her over, bending her at the waist. Sweet Jesus, what a sight. Her creamy skin. The two perfect globes of her ass.

And her gorgeous pussy, pretty and perfect and so obviously recently fucked. I moaned and lined my cock up against her. Then I slowly plunged all the way in.

She gasped and I stopped. I didn't want to. But there was no way in hell I was going to hurt her again.

"Am I hurting you?"

She looked over her shoulder at me and shook her head. She was so fucking beautiful it almost hurt to look at her. I had wanted to touch her since the moment I laid eyes on her.

Touch her... that was a laugh. I wanted everything from her. I wanted to take everything and give everything too.

And now, I was doing exactly what I wanted.

"Good."

I reached down and found her clit, teasing it a little. I grimaced as she clenched down on me, hugging my shaft with her hot, sticky sweetness.

"Because I'm not even close to being done."

I knelt down on one leg behind her and started pumping into her, hard and steady. She arched her back, trying to wiggle against me. I held her hips firmly in place so I could work my cock as deep as I wanted.

The sight of my big hands on her perfect ass was almost too much for me. I started to fuck her a little faster. Her body clasped mine, tugging at me every time I started to pull out.

Jesus fucking Christ she felt good!

I felt my balls getting even heavier. The damn things felt like lead weights. I knew if I let myself come inside her again it was risky. She could get knocked up.

Good.

I reached down and stroked her sensitive little nub again. When I came, I wanted her coming too. She gasped and her sexy little hips jerked.

"Connor... Oh!"

"That's it sweetheart. Pull it out of me."

She moaned, clearly incoherent. I felt her start to convulse around my shaft and I lost it. I thrust into her hard and fast, my finger barely able to keep tempo on her clit.

But it was enough. It was more than enough.

She screamed as we came together, cock and pussy and sweat and juices exploding in a moment of pure fucking ecstasy.

"FUCK!"

I couldn't stop pumping my cock into her. Couldn't stop the out of control bucking of my hips. I hoped I wasn't hurting her tender flesh but I couldn't slow down. There was nothing I could do to stop, as I poured all my pent up heat and frustration into her grasping little pussy.

"Oh GOD!"

I collapsed forward with a moan. I was still inside her, my hands braced on the bed. She was such a tiny little thing, fitting underneath my body so sweetly. I curved over her, feeling my shaft pump out the last few drops.

My lips found the tender spot between her neck and her shoulder and rained kisses down on her. Even her neck was perfect. Graceful and slender... the skin so soft... the scent of her hair so sweet.

I licked her shoulder, just to get a taste. Hmmm... she was pretty much perfect everywhere.

She shivered and I felt her little pussy clamping down on my cock as she had tiny little orgasms...

aftershocks. I played with her nipples a bit, wondering how long I could keep this exquisite fucking cock massage going.

And just like that, the beast was getting hard again.

CASSANDRA

hat are you-"

"Shhh... I'm taking you to the shower."

"Oh, that sounds nice."

I snuggled against his wide, strong chest as he carried me to the bathroom. Unlike the rest of the house, it was clearly new. The bathroom was uber luxurious with a huge walk-in shower and dark gray and sage green tiles.

"Wow."

He smiled at me and reached into the shower. He held me with one arm without the slightest effort. That's how strong he was.

"It's the only thing I bothered with when I moved in."

"It's... amazing."

He set me on my feet in the shower and kissed me softly as the steam started to rise around us. I leaned into the kiss, letting my lips part. He nipped my bottom lip and pulled back.

"Careful."

"Why?"

"You don't want to rile me up, sweetheart."

I blushed.

"I can do that by kissing you?"

He gave me an incredulous look.

"You can do that by breathing. Now turn around, I'm going to wash your back."

I did as he asked, bracing my hands against the shower wall. I sighed as his big calloused hands rubbed my skin. He was extremely thorough, staring with my shoulders and working his way down.

All the way down.

He rubbed my bottom and I giggled. He slapped my ass lightly and told me to be a good girl. Then he washed my thighs and calves.

"Lift."

I raised my foot and he washed that too, sudsing between every toe. I giggled a little, wondering if he planned on sucking them again and was planning ahead. He washed the other foot and then turned me around to face him.

My eyes got wide as I stared at his perfect body. His perfect, extremely *erect* body.

His gorgeous cock was standing straight up.

His gaze was hot as he lifted me. He set me under the rain fall shower head. I gasped as the soap slid off of me all at once.

"Ohhh…"

He grinned.

"Now I'm going to do the front."

I was out of breath as I watched him pour shower gel into his palms. He started at my neck. He was extra thorough with my breasts, tugging on my nipples and grunting his approval as they got hard under his nimble fingers.

He washed my belly and my thighs, not touching between my legs. I wiggled a bit in protest and he shushed me.

"You don't need any soap there, sweetie. Don't need it."

Then he knelt and washed the front of my legs. I watched him work, even more turned-on than I'd been before. He smiled faintly as his face came closer to my pussy. He licked me and I moaned, my hands in his hair.

But he stopped too soon. He stood and turned me so the water washed over my front.

"Hmm... Connor... I want..."

He chuckled and his hands cupped my breasts. His hardness pressed against my bottom.

"Sorry love, we both have to wait. I was already too rough with you."

I bit my lip, pouting.

"Why don't you let me wash you then?"

"Sweetheart... not now."

He caught my hand and kissed it. I pouted a little and he bit my fingertip, making me squeal.

"If you touch me right now, I'm going to lose it."

"I don't mind."

"You are delicate down there, sweetheart. I don't want to hurt your sweet little pussy."

I leaned back and watched him wash himself quickly. He shook himself like a dog at the end and I laughed. Then he wrapped me in a towel and started drying me off.

"I can do that, Conn."

"I know. Just let me have my fun. I want to take care of you Casey..."

He smiled at me sheepishly and I realized he meant it. He wanted to do everything for me. I nodded and he dried me off, wrapping a fresh towel around me at the end.

Then he kissed me.

"I'm getting wet again!"

He grinned and scooped me up, carrying me to his bed. He put me under the covers and stood there, staring down at me.

"You sleep in here from now on."

"Where are you sleeping?"

"In here. But not tonight. I don't trust myself."

He grinned.

"Besides I have work to do."

I snuggled underneath the covers and gave him a coy look.

"But what if I get cold? Who will warm me up?"

He moaned, looking like he was in pain.

"Don't tease me, sweetheart. You're going to be sore as it is."

He leaned down and pressed a kiss to my forehead.

"Get some sleep."

CONNOR

I heard the chain hit the floor and smiled. She was up. I stretched from where I'd been standing at the kitchen island.

My email was full, rapid fire information coming in now. I'd been on and off half the night and into the morning. But I shut the laptop anyway, too eager to get back upstairs.

I'd come down a few minutes ago to make breakfast. I'd been checking in on her, watching her sleep throughout night. I was hoping she'd wake up since dawn, wondering if it was too soon to have her again.

My little angel was so small, and it had been her first time after all. I wasn't a wild animal. Or at least, I was trying not to be.

I poured her a cup of coffee and carried it upstairs.

Her hair was wild and wavy as she clutched a sheet to her breasts. I felt my cock lurch towards her, just from a glimpse of those tempting curves and soft skin.

Her face was soft from sleep, her lips looking full and oh-so-kissable.

Her eyes on the other hand, were a different matter.

My little angel was pissed.

"You chained me again?"

I nodded, smiling at the indignant look on her beautiful face.

"I made you coffee. And the griddle is warmed up if you're hungry."

Though I had turned the gas off again... just in case we took a while to get downstairs. I was trying to be thoughtful, while planning for the best possible outcome. More bed time with Casey.

Hopefully, right now.

She took the coffee and sniffed it, giving me an irritated look. She was so cute when she was annoyed with me. But she took a sip anyway.

"Griddle?"

"Flapjacks sweetie."

"Oh."

She set the coffee down and looked at me.

"What's with the chain? Is this a kinky sex game?"

I stayed where I was, my arms crossed over my chest.

"No. But it could be."

She perked up a bit at that. I almost laughed at the same time as my dick got even harder. She was so fucking adorable. I loved how curious she was about sex.

She wasn't overly shy. She didn't have any hang ups. Or experience. She just needed some lessons. And bless her heart, she was more than eager to learn.

I'd decided the moment I saw her that I was going to be the one to teach her.

Only me. *Ever.*

No other man would touch her again.

I walked across the room and stood over the bed.

"Lay back for me."

She blinked and did as I asked. I pulled the sheet away, admiring the long lines of her body. She was so delicately feminine, and strong at the same time.

"Spread your legs."

She blushed a little and did as I asked. I grazed the back of my hand over her sweet pussy and she whimpered softly. I leaned down and pressed a gentle kiss on her lips as I circled her clit with my thumb.

"How does this feel?"

She closed her eyes and moaned softly. Her tight little pussy was already getting wet. She was so fucking responsive.

Our breath commingled as I stayed where I was, our lips less than an inch apart, my fingers busy below. I slid a finger inside her, watching her face carefully.

"Did I hurt you last night?"

She shook her head breathlessly, her hips rising to meet my fingers. I pulled my hand away and blew softly on her pussy lips.

"Are you sure? You're not sore at all?"

She whimpered and lifted her hips. My cock almost exploded at the sight of her gorgeous untouched pussy.

Well, mostly untouched.

"Just a little…"

"I want to fuck you now. But if it hurts you have to tell me. There are other things we can do."

"There are?"

I smirked at her and licked her pussy lips bottom to top. I flicked my tongue against her clit and she squealed like a little bird.

"Don't you remember your book?"

We'd left off right before the submissive gave head to the 'master.' I knew she'd never done that before and it would probably kill me to let her try, but it would be worth it.

"You mean- like a blowjob?"

I moaned and kept licking her outer lips. They were pink but not red. I hoped she could take another pounding or two because I wanted to fuck her about fifty ways from Sunday.

"Yes. I mean like a blowjob."

"Hmmm... I want to do that to you Connor. Can I try?"

She was offering to- oh my God. I cursed and pushed myself away from her. She was turned-on and so eager to experiment. I knew it was going to be challenging for her. I was so big and she was so small. I stared at her plump lips as she licked them, looking nervous but excited.

Who was I to say no?

"Okay."

I stretched out on my back, in my track pants and an open shirt. My cock was making the biggest fucking tent I'd seen since I went to the circus as a kid. I pressed down on it and moaned in anticipation.

She leaned on her side and reached for me. I grunted as she caressed me through the slinky fabric. I was going to pop, and soon.

It didn't matter that she had no idea what she was doing. Or how small her hands were. Or her soft lips...

I exhaled as she tugged my pants down, biting her lip in concentration. Her perfect tits brushed my belly as I lifted my hips and helped her slide my pants down.

My cock bounced in the air, finally free. She gripped it and smiled. Her silky light brown hair caressed my stomach as she leaned closer and-

"Hmmfff…"

Her soft lips brushed my tip as her hot tongue swirled against it. Holy fucking shit. If that was a sign of things to come… well, this was going to be a very short lesson.

"Tell me what to do."

"That's good. You can lick it a little more- oh Christ!"

I tangled my hands in her hair as she tongued me again. She glanced up at me, her lips hovering just above my cock.

"Is that bad?"

"No. You didn't do anything wrong. The only bad thing you can do is teeth." I tried to smile but I felt like I was going to explode. This was the most erotic thing that had happened to me in my entire life. "Anything else goes."

"Oh. Okay."

She started again, licking me like an ice cream cone. I moaned, realizing she was imitating me when I'd used my mouth on her. Christ, if she kept up those soft light licks I would die of a case of blue balls.

"You can, take it in your mouth and- unfff- suck on it."

"Hmmm? Okay."

She pulled me into her mouth and sucked. Her tongue fluttered at the tip a bit and my hips jerked.

"You can go a little deeper- yes- fucking hell- yes- just like that. Now do that a few times, up and down."

She bobbed her head up and down on my cock and I cursed. It felt too good. I was going to come. And soon.

She stopped, her fingers grazing my sac.

"What about these?"

"Hmmfff- you can touch them or lick them. Christ, I'm going to come soon."

"You are?"

She stared up at me, her fingers tracing soft circles on my heavy nuts. I nodded and she leaned down and licked my balls. I clenched my hands into fists as she delicately ran her tongue over my sac. I heaved a sigh of relief when she took my shaft into her mouth again a few minutes later.

"You can- oh Christ I'm so close- you can swallow it when I come. Or I can take over and use my hand. It's up to you."

She murmured something around my cock and I told her again I would warn her, and not to stop, dear lord, please do not stop...

"Unffff! Now! I'm coming now!"

I hissed as she teased the come out, sucking at my cock with her hot little lips and tongue. And she swallowed it.

God bless her, she swallowed it down.

I held her head, trying not to be too rough as my hips jerked. My cock slid even deeper into her throat as the hot stream continued exploding from my tip.

She kept sucking, kept swallowing until she pulled the last drops from my flesh. I fell back on the bed, staring at the ceiling.

Jesus Christ.

A blowjob virgin had just given me the best head of my life.

Not just slightly better. Miles better. Fucking galaxies better than anything I'd ever felt before.

Well, other than fucking her of course. And I was going to do that again soon too. I just needed to catch my breath…

She sat up and smiled at me. I reached for her and took her hand, tugging her against me. When I could finally speak a few minutes later I told her how special she was. How amazing.

"I am?"

"Yes, you are. Come here sweetheart."

She curled against my chest and I sighed, the feeling of her in my arms so perfect it was overwhelming. I felt something inside me crack open.

I slid my hand down her back to her bottom and she wiggled a little, making me chuckle.

My little wildcat was still horny. I hadn't finished her off when I'd been tasting her before.

Daddy could take care of that for her.

"Lay back sweetie, I want to taste you." She blushed and stared up at me. I squeezed her waist. "Go on, be a good girl."

She leaned back on the bed and I moved between her thighs. She was breathless and wide-eyed as I grinned at her, checking out her sexy body as I slid down her body, kissing all her yummy little bits.

I stared at her, shaking my head in awe. Every inch of her was perfect. She looked fucking amazing from every angle.

I bet she even looked good upside down. I tried to picture fucking her in a wheelbarrow position, with her hands on the floor and her legs in my hands as I took her from behind. Maybe we'd try that later too. I wanted to try *everything*.

But first things first.

I had a naughty little kitty to tend to.

And I wanted to make her scream.

I pulled her legs over my shoulders and stared at that sweet little pussy. I was hard again and I wanted in. But since I knew I had to go easy on her today, I decided to drag it out as much as possible.

I was going to make my little angel beg. Beg me using dirty words. The filthier the better.

"Tell me what you want sweetheart."

"I want you to… um…"

I smiled, my face hovering over her pussy.

"Lick you?"

"Yes."

"Tell me."

"I want you to lick me. Please."

I slid my tongue up and down the edge of her puffy little lips, teasing her.

"Like that?"

"Hmm… yes, please."

"What else?"

I slid my finger up to her clit and waited.

"Touch me. Do that thing you did before."

"You want me to rub your naughty little clit? Like this?"

She mumbled something incoherent as my finger traced her clit.

"Yes, but…"

"But what?"

"Can you do it… a little faster?"

"Like this?"

I circled her clit rapidly and her hips jerked.

"You want my tongue in your little pussy at the same time?"

"Yes! Hmmm yes. Please."

"Tell me, Casey. Tell me you want me to fuck you with my tongue and rub your needy little clit."

I slid my tongue just outside her opening and she whimpered, reaching for me. I smiled at her patiently, waiting.

"Oh! Please- um- oh God- please fuck me with your tongue and-"

I slid a finger inside her and lapped my tongue on her clit.

"Say my name."

"Connor!"

"Suck my clit, Connor."

She didn't answer so I switched again, licking her clit and gently fingering her below.

She was moaning as I toyed with her, doing a bit of this and a bit of that. I could tell she was beyond words. But I was having way too much fun to take mercy on her.

Besides I wanted her to come at the exact moment I slid into her. I wasn't going to be able to wait much longer, so I wanted her as frantic and as close as possible.

My cock pressed into the mattress as I drove both of us completely fucking insane for the next ten minutes. The room was silent, other than my sounds of appreciation and her eager little whimpers of pleasure.

I stopped and stared up at her, my fingers stroking her lightly.

"Do you want me to fuck you now?"

She nodded and moaned with her eyes shut. That was going to have to be enough. I could tell she was out of her mind.

I lined my cock up with her and rubbed the tip up and down her slick lips. I tapped her clit with it and she whimpered. The way she looked, laying there, open and wild and desperate for me...

Well, let's just say I forgot to be gentle.

I slid into her with a curse. All the way in. I braced my body with my arms straight on either side of her. My hips took over, mindlessly fucking her hard and slow. It wasn't sweet or tender. I'd waited all night for this.

I grunted with each thrust as I pistoned my cock in and out of her. My tempo increased steadily with each stroke. And just like I'd planned, Casey came almost instantly.

She shook and shimmied all over the bed, her pussy creaming all over my cock. I didn't stop though. Couldn't stop.

All I could do was make sure we orgasmed together when the time came. I leaned down and pulled her nipple into my mouth, sucking hard as my rhythm increased again.

I was close now. On the edge. But not quite ready to let go.

"Fuck!"

I grabbed her and lifted her, slamming her back against the heavy wood headboard. I wrapped her legs around my waist, holding her ass with one hand as I pounded her harder and harder.

"Oh God! Christ! I'm going to-"

I roared like an animal as my cock expanded inside her. She was coming still, trapped in an endless orgasm. She cried out as she peaked again. Her body pulled at me in a way that made me fucking explode.

Every inch of my body was alive. The headboard banged against the wall again and again until I was spent. It seemed to go on forever.

I kissed her as her body convulsed on my cock. I held perfectly still, impaling her to the headboard. She was suspended there, like a pretty little butterfly on a pin.

I reached down and smiled at her as I pressed on her clit. She screamed and came again. I grunted as my cock got squeezed. I fucking loved it though. She was milking me for every drop and I fucking loved it.

Gently, I lifted her off my cock and we slid to the bed in a tangle of exhausted limbs. I realized pancakes were going to have to wait as I drifted into a deep sleep.

C*reak...*

I blinked, realizing something was wrong. Someone was here. They'd just come up the stairs and opened the bedroom door. And they weren't being quiet about it.

I opened my eyes slowly, seeing two people standing in the doorway. I rolled to the side, pulling my body in front of Casey's as I reached for my gun.

I'd fucked up. I'd let my guard down. They'd come after her and now I had to keep her alive.

No matter what the cost. I'd gladly risk my life for hers. She was mine and I was going to protect her dammit.

"Connor Jason DeWitt."

I lowered the gun at the familiar voice, throwing the safety. I blinked as the room came into focus. My mother and my sister were standing in the open doorway, staring at me in shock.

Well, my mother was in shock. My little sister Kelly was looking at me with a shit-eating grin.

"Conn? Why is there a girl chained to your bed?"

CASSANDRA

"Help me. Please help me. He's kept me chained up here for days."

Connor shot me a look of pure disbelief and I laughed. He looked so miserable. I knew instantly that the woman standing there was his mother.

"Connor! Did you kidnap this girl?"

He turned around and pulled his pants on. I knew I should be embarrassed, and I was. But this was too funny for words.

Connor looked positively mortified. He pointed at me and I grinned.

"Not one word!"

"Did he kidnap you?"

"He did." I smiled. "But I forgive him."

The younger girl looked at me and laughed. The older woman looked scandalized. Connor looked furious.

"Casey, stow it. Mom, Kelly. This is Casey. Soon to be my wife."

"What?"

"WHAT?"

I sat up, forgetting to be embarrassed. He winked at me and tossed me a shirt.

"Did you really think I was letting you go after all that?"

"But-"

He raised an eyebrow.

"Be good and I'll unchain you."

I sputtered and crossed my arms, saying nothing. Of all the high handed-

He wanted to marry me.

I smiled suddenly, as he unlocked the cuff on my leg. He gave me a surly look. I leaned forward to whisper to him.

"How are you going to explain this to them? Locking up an innocent girl for your kinky sex games?"

He pinched my bottom and I squeaked.

"You're a bad girl."

"Does that mean I don't get pancakes?"

"No, I'll feed you." He grinned suddenly. "You're going to need your strength for later. For my revenge."

My jaw dropped as he stood and walked away, whistling. He put an arm around his mom and sister and led them away.

"Come on, let's give my fiance some privacy to get dressed."

"My clothes are downstairs!"

He smiled at me over his shoulder. I crossed my arms and sat there, waiting. A few minutes later the shopping bags slid into the room.

"What about-"

"Get dressed."

I gave up, looking through the bags again. I hadn't even tried any of this stuff on! But my bags were downstairs so...

I pulled out a bra and pantie set in hot pink lace and smiled. If he thought he was the only one getting revenge, he was sorely mistaken.

I rinsed off quickly in the shower and put on the sexy underthings. Then I pulled out a light blue pair of stretch jeans, a cute v-neck top in dark green and a pair of brown suede ankle booties.

How the heck had he gotten all my sizes right?

He must have looked at my stuff downstairs while I slept, checking labels and what not. I shook my head, glancing in the mirror. He'd even gotten me some cherry flavored lipgloss and vanilla body spray.

I combed my damp hair and shrugged. The man had surprisingly good taste in clothes. I looked pretty classy, compared to the usual gear I wore to the bar or for hanging around the house.

Not bad, Cass.

I swallowed, suddenly nervous. I'd been laughing before but now things were different. Now it was time to meet the mother.

CONNOR

"Sheila is on her way."

"What?"

"She was worried about you! We all were!

"Mom, this is not good. Casey isn't supposed to be here."

"Well, how was I supposed to know that?" My mother frowned and pointed a finger at me. "You never call in sick!"

"I want to hear about the girl."

"You're not helping Kelly."

My little sister gave me a cheeky grin and I rolled my eyes, deciding to ignore her. I heated the griddle back up and pulled out the pancake batter.

"What are you doing?"

"I need to feed my fiance."

"You mean your captive? What the hell is going on here Connor?"

"It's a long story mom."

"Are you really going to marry a person you just met?"

"I didn't *just* meet her, mom. And yes."

"Well, I think she seems nice."

210

I glared at Kelly.

"You would. The two of you are both trouble makers."

"Wait, you're marrying her and you don't think she's nice?"

I sighed and poured batter onto the hissing surface.

"Yes, I think she's nice. But that's not why-"

A loud throat clearing came from behind me and I turned. *Well, Goddamn.* My eyes slowly took in the sight of Casey Jones, looking extra foxy.

No PJ's. No greasy bar uniform. She looked like a woman.

She looked fucking amazing.

It was a good thing I'd decided to lock her down before some other guy tried to snatch her up. Because she was even more desirable than I'd even realized. And that was saying something.

"Your pancakes are burning."

Casey smiled and crossed her arms over her chest.

"You were saying?"

I stood there like an idiot, staring at her with my tongue out, holding a spatula.

A domestic idiot, but an idiot. Casey cleared her throat, arching a brow.

"What?"

"Why you were marrying me?"

"Did he even ask you?"

"No, he didn't."

"Shut up, Kelly."

I flipped the pancakes and got out some plates.

"Are you two eating?" My mom shook her head and Kelly popped a stray pancake crumb into her mouth.

"Nope."

I made two plates and carried them over to the coffee table. I coughed and tossed Casey's dirty book onto the couch. Kelly, unfortunately had to say something about it.

"Oh I love that book! Mom, did you read this one yet?"

I started laughing as my mom turned beet red. Casey sat down beside me, giving me a cute but cranky look. I kissed her cheek. I wanted to do a whole hell of a lot more but we had company.

"Eat. Someone's coming and things are about to get dicey."

"Who?"

I sighed, wondering if I should get her the hell out of here.

"One of the people I work with. An agent."

Casey jumped up, panic all over her beautiful face.

"You said no one knew where you lived!"

I grabbed her before she could run.

"Calm down. She's trustworthy. I'm going to protect you. I promised you and I meant it."

She stared at me, her huge eyes wide. Reality had just crashed our little party and I didn't much like it.

"How? How can you protect me?"

"Let me worry about that."

Slowly she sat down again.

My mother raised her eyebrows. Kelly too.

"I guess this explains the chain."

I nodded.

"Yes, it does." I cut up a piece of pancakes and held it in front of Casey's gorgeous lips.

"Now, eat."

CASSANDRA

"I'm keeping her."

Sheila looked furious. The older agent was fond of Connor, that much was obvious. Maybe that's why she was so mad.

He was infuriating sometimes. But so cute. But also infuriating.

Like for example, it was a little weird that Conn kept talking about me like I was a damn pet.

"You're a damn fool, you know that?" She sighed, looking like she was giving up. "You're smarter than this, Conn."

He gave her a wry smile.

"Apparently, I'm not."

I chewed the edge of a slice of grapefruit. The last thing left from the extremely late breakfast that Connor had cooked for me.

Then he hovered over me while he watched me eat. He slung an arm over my shoulders, encouraging me to eat every last bite.

His mother and sister had peppered me with questions. I could tell they wanted to get to know me. But I had so little to tell.

They asked about my childhood. Where I was from. What I did.

Ha. Ha. Ha.

Connor had told them to can it, in pretty much those exact words. I'd been grateful to be let off the hook. I already felt ashamed of my past. 'Less than' somehow. I wasn't a normal girl my age, with a loving family who was headed off to college, or even close to graduating by now.

I wasn't that lucky.

But in some ways I was *luckier*. I'd had it all, lost it, and been saved. I thanked my lucky stars everyday that Mason had taken me in. A big, mean looking biker with a heart of gold.

How do you explain that to two nice suburban ladies?

So I didn't even try. I made small talk and ate. Basically, feeling like a big dork. Conn had done his best to make me at ease, wrapping his arm around me, feeding me, teasing me about this and that while his mother stared at me suspiciously.

And then Sheila had walked in.

I shook my head. For a bachelor, Connor sure had a lot of women in his life. I watched as the older woman glared at Conn, then at me, then at Conn again.

"You are out of your Goddamn mind."

She kept insulting him and threatening to call it in. He kept asking her for time. Then she said something that made my blood run cold.

"Mason never even mentioned she was missing when you brought him in!"

I looked back and forth between them.

"Mason is under investigation?"

Connor shook his head.

"No. He was."

I stood up. "What the fuck Connor?" I grabbed my backpack and headed for the door. Besos followed me, whimpering for attention. Connor stepped in front of me and shook his head.

"Forget it. Not happening."

"I need to see him!"

"He refused protection. He's not in custody. I have guys on him."

"Tell me what is going on then!"

I poked his chest and he held his hands up in surrender. Sheila laughed and shook her head.

"I have seen everything now. I changed my mind Connor. You deserve her."

"Can it, Sheil." Connor rubbed his hands up and down my arms. "I told you, he's not in danger. *You* are. So-"

"Actually, that was why I was looking for her."

We both turned to look at Sheila. She chewed the inside of her cheek for a minute, like she was deciding something.

"Your little waitress here isn't the only one missing now." She looked hard at Connor, then at me. "We lost track of Dante. He hasn't been seen in 48 hours."

I grimaced and made a sound of disgust. "He's probably in a basement somewhere, torturing someone." Conn looked at me, his eyebrow raised.

"What? I said I knew him."

"I didn't realize you knew him that well."

"He took a shine to me."

Connor stepped closer, his eyes boring into mine. He looked dangerous suddenly. Like someone was threatening something that belonged to him.

It wasn't hard to figure out what that something was.

Me.

"A shine?"

"Nothing happened Conn! Jesus, I told you I avoided the guy."

"But it is not beyond the realm of possibility that he might have sent you blood splattered roses." He paused, his jaw ticking. "Even if you *hadn't* witnessed a murder."

And there it was. He'd said it and I couldn't think of a damn thing to say. I just stared at him, my eyes wide.

"Maybe."

He nodded and turned away.

"That's what I thought."

"Conn, if she's a witness she should be in custody."

"She *is* in custody. Mine." He exhaled and leaned against the kitchen island. "And she's not a witness."

"But-"

"She didn't see anything, Sheil. Forget it."

I nearly fell over. I was sitting here, watching one federal agent tell another one to ignore the truth. The truth that was staring every single person in the room in the face.

Connor was breaking about fifty laws trying to protect me. He had since the moment he'd taken me to his house and chained me up.

And he was doing it all for me.

CONNOR

"Thanks Sheil. I'll be in later."

I waved as everyone left. Finally. My shell-shocked mother, my giggling sister, and the woman who pretty much held my career in her hands.

But she said she would keep Casey in her back pocket. Not say anything. Not get my ass kicked out of the department for gross misconduct.

For now, anyway.

I turned and crossed my arms, locking the door behind me. Casey crossed her arms too. We stared at each other, each of us pissed off.

But for very different reasons.

"Can you cook?"

She blinked at me, then nodded. "Yeah, some stuff. Why?"

"Because I'm starving." I held up the chain. "And it's time to pay the piper."

Her eyes got bigger as I started stripping. She shook her head and pointed at me.

"You are not tying me up again!"

I smiled grimly.

"Oh yes, I fucking am. I'm tired of running after your ass every time you get a bee in your bonnet."

I distracted her by taking my pants off. My cock bobbed free, pointing right at her. Hard and ready. I squeezed it, feeling my heavy nuts swing.

"A bee in my what?"

She was staring at my cock, clearly not focused on the conversation at hand. I had to admit, I loved that awestruck look in her eyes. I grinned and reached for her.

"Bonnet."

I kissed her deeply, sliding my tongue into her mouth. I started peeling her clothes off. I cursed as I saw the hot pink lace underthings I'd bought her. My cock swelled even larger.

"Christ, those are hot."

"Huh?"

"I like your panties."

"Oh- you got them for me."

I smiled at her. She was already in a sex daze. I loved how easily I did that to her.

"I know."

I ran my hands over her flanks and up again. Her skin was silky smooth. I peeled down her panties, kissing my way down her body as I stripped off the last little scrap between me and my goal.

Then I snapped the cuff on her ankle.

"What the hell Conn!"

I smiled up at her and ran my hands up between her legs.

"What's wrong?"

She gasped as I toyed with her soft little pussy lips. I leaned forward and licked her, flicking my tongue against her clit.

"You- bastard- oh…."

She quieted right down, thinking I was going to take care of her. But I had no intention of letting her come. Not yet. Not for a good long while.

I was still pissed at her for messing with me this morning.

"I'm so hungry. Let's make something to eat."

"Huh?"

She looked adorably confused as I stood up and pecked her cheek. Then I walked into the kitchen and tied an apron around my waist.

"You want to- cook? Now?"

"Aren't you hungry?" I smiled at her, my eyes between her thighs. "I know I am."

She just stared at me in a trance. I shrugged and got out some steak and fished around for something green in the crisper drawer. I had a bag of broccoli in the back. Perfect.

"Wash this."

I held out the grocery bag and she walked over and took it. Then I got the steak going in a cast iron skillet, seasoning it with salt and pepper.

I flipped the steak a few times to sear it and turned the heat down.

I leaned back against the counter to enjoy the show. Casey's slender back curved down to that ridiculously squeezable ass. I licked my lips as she bent over the sink. She set the broccoli on a cutting board and looked over her shoulder at me.

"Done."

"Here."

I handed her a knife from the box of confiscated sharps. She started neatly trimming the ends of the broccoli and cutting the rough parts of the stems.

Good girl.

I stepped up behind her and started kissing her neck as I fondled her perfect breasts.

"Pay attention, sweetheart. Good. Now fill that pot with water. Hmm hmmm…"

She moaned as I lifted my hands away, but just to put the pot on the stove. I dumped the veggies in, added salt and pepper and covered it with a lid.

Then I got down to business.

Casey squealed as I lifted her up and plopped her fine ass on the island. I grinned and pushed her back so she was lying flat, her legs hanging over the edge.

Then I spread her legs wide and stared at that gorgeous pussy of hers.

Scratch that. It was my pussy now dammit.

"Just a little snack…"

She whimpered as I tasted her. Lick by lick. I didn't apply nearly enough pressure to be satisfying. I just teased her.

Then I smelled the steak starting to burn.

"Times up."

I turned the stove off and helped her down, unable to resist one more taste. I put one steak and some veggies on a plate and sat down at the table.

"On my lap. I'll feed you."

She gave me a piqued look. I just waited. Finally she sat down, the thin fabric of the apron the only thing between us.

"Good girl."

I cut the steak and broccoli into small pieces. I made a perfect bite with a bit of each and held the fork to her lips. I watched closely as she pulled the food into her mouth and chewed.

Hmmfff… that was hot.

I took a bite and then gave her another. She wiggled around on my lap while we ate the first steak.

"Behave."

She tossed her hair over her shoulder and pouted. I slipped one hand between her legs and bit her neck.

"Are you still hungry?"

"I'll get the other steak-"

"No. Not the steak."

She blinked her eyes as she got the message. She licked her lips and I could see she was going to do what I asked. I leaned back and waited.

Thankfully, I didn't have to wait long.

I stared as she slipped between my legs, the chain rattling on the floor. She stared up at me as she lifted the apron and grasped my cock with her soft hand.

I watched in awe as she pulled me into her mouth and started sucking me, her lips rolling up and down my shaft like a Goddamn pro.

Fuck!

"Slower."

Her gorgeous blue eyes stared up at me as she slowed her tempo, her tongue licking the edge of my tip with each stroke. I gripped my hands in her hair, guiding her further down my shaft.

I knew I was close. Just seeing her down there, worshipping my cock, it was enough to make me explode.

Not yet.

"That's good, sweetheart- hmmfff- you're going to want to stop-"

She looked up at me in question and I lifted her. In one smooth motion I had her on my lap, her legs dangling over my thighs.

I grinned at the shocked look on her face as I lowered her onto my cock. I groaned as I was able to get just inside her tight little pussy lips.

"That's it, sweetheart. Just relax and open for me..."

She whimpered, her fingernails scraping my shoulders. I was hypnotized by the sight of my shaft stretching her wide. Her perky round tits were tantalizingly close so I leaned forward and licked one. She gasped, and I was able to slide a little further in.

"Jesus! That's it, Casey. Let me in."

I squeezed her juicy ass checks in my hands and started thrusting upwards. I was careful not to fuck her too hard.

Not yet.

She was probably still too tender.

She squeezed down on me, her walls wrapping my cock in a hot and slippery hug. That was it. Her body opened up to me like a flower. I moaned as I watched my cock slide all the way in.

"Hold on tight, sweetheart."

Then I went to town.

CASSANDRA

Connor lifted me up and down like a rag doll.

He stared between our bodies, watching his thick cock disappear inside me.

He let go with one hand and licked his finger, lowering it to my clit.

Just like that, after all the teasing, I came. My whole body shook as he grinned at me, lifting me up and down with one hand. He watched my face as I came, then stared back down between us.

"So good baby... so fucking good..."

He started pumping his hips up, holding me down against them as he fucked me deep and hard. It was like he couldn't get close enough. He wanted to be as far inside me as possible.

He groaned and I felt it- the tingle that started when he was about to come. I felt my body answer his, clenching down on him as I started to convulse.

My skin felt hot and then cold as shivers ran through me. He held me down on his cock, my thighs wide, my pussy completely open to him.

He was cursing and grunting like a wild animal as his cock shot his seed straight up inside me. I felt it fill me up, even more than any of the other times.

And that was saying something.

He slowed his thrusts and his hands flexed on my hips. He pressed me down even harder. I couldn't have gotten away if I wanted to, never mind the cuff around my ankle.

"Sweetheart…"

"Hmmm?"

"You're going to kill me with sex."

"I am?"

"Yes. Oh fuck- yeah, squeeze me like that-" He groaned as I felt my pussy squeezed down on him instinctively. "It's not usually like this."

"It's not?"

He laughed, the sound rough and hard and cynical.

"No. It's not. Not even close."

"Oh."

I blushed as he continued to stare down at the place our bodies joined. I was still trembling when I felt it.

Conn was hard again inside me. And getting harder.

"Are you-"

"Yes, baby. I want to have you again."

"Already?"

"Yes." He moaned, brushing my hair away from my face. "Already. Always."

I wiggled and he cursed.

"Shit. I don't want to hurt you Case-"

"I'm fine."

He stared at me, his eyes hard. He didn't believe me.

"You're so small baby and I'm-"

"I'm fine."

He growled and lifted me up, wrapping my legs around him. I gasped as he pushed me up against the post in the middle of the floor. He started fucking me hard and fast.

It was surreal being held up in the air like that- speared by his cock. It felt so good I knew I was going come again soon.

"I should- uh- chain you up- uh- right here."

I moaned and my head fell back. He lowered his head to my throat and kissed it.

Then he bit it, his hot breath fanning my neck.

RING RING.

"Fuck if I'm getting that."

RING RING.

He kept riding me, taking me standing up like a beast. I dug my nails into his back as another phone somewhere else in the house starting going off.

RING RING.

"FUCK!"

He slowed his thrusts, leaning his forehead against mine. He kissed me hard and pulled out. I was quiet as he lowered me and wiped his brow.

"Shit, I'm sorry."

"It's okay."

I didn't want to stop, don't get me wrong. But he was already grabbing his phone, and answering it with a terse 'DeWitt.'

He stared at me, nodding and agreeing with whatever was being said on the other end of the line. He hung up and reached for his clothes.

"I have to go sweetie. You're going to have to wait for round two."

He grabbed his gun and badge and kissed me hard.

"Fuck, I don't want to go."

"It's okay. You have to do your job. It's important."

"You're right. I know you're right."

"But Conn?"

He brushed my hair back and kissed my neck, his hand sliding down to my ass to squeeze it.

"Yes, sweetheart?"

"You might want to put on some shoes."

MASON

"If you don't fucking produce Casey, I'm going to fucking come after you."

I slammed the phone down, not the least bit concerned that I'd just threatened a federal agent. I was standing behind the bar of The Jar, leaning against the solid wood.

The old polished wood usually comforted me. Reminded me that I'd done good. I'd gotten out.

Well, kinda.

And now my stupid ass decision to let the fucking Hell Raisers in the front door had put Case in trouble. Worse than trouble. She was in danger.

Fuck me.

The girl was far too old to be my daughter but damn it, she *was* family. I loved her like a little sister. A feisty, pain in the ass, worrying me to the bone, little sister.

She'd broken my heart the day I found her, standing out in the rain like a half-drowned puppy. I'd recognized myself in the girl's sheer determination to survive, and the look of utter desolation in her beautiful, sad eyes.

The stubborn pride too.

I'd taken her in and never looked back.

And I was going to fucking protect her!

The only thing keeping me sane was the fact that I knew Connor was an up and up guy. He was a boy scout and a cowboy rolled into one. Plus, I'd seen the look in his eyes when he talked about promising her he'd protect me.

He was gonzo.

Finished.

A marked man.

Wherever Casey was, I was pretty sure she had him wrapped around her cute little finger.

I hoped she was making him suffer. Didn't matter though. The man owed me an explanation.

And I wanted to see her. Know she was safe.

Plus, the man had my damn dog and cats! The house had been so quiet last night. I didn't like it.

Knowing there was an unmarked vehicle out front hadn't helped much either. And that everyone in the damn state knew I was being watched by the Feds.

I popped the top off a beer and took a deep pull. I was tempted to have something stronger but hell, I needed my wits about me. Besides, beer was pretty much like water to me at this point in my life.

Oh yeah. I'd been a bad boy growing up. Very bad.

But I'd spent years trying to make up for it. To do something good. To erase the memories that haunted me to this very fucking day.

It was early, just after the lunch crowd thinned out. Normal folks came in here for the insanely good barbecue. My own personal secret recipe.

But I was not expecting Shane, the Raisers' new VP to come waltzing in here in broad fucking daylight. The smug bastard held up his hands and opened his jacket to show me he was unarmed.

I scowled as he sauntered up to the bar like he owned the place. He was too pretty by far. And he'd come out of nowhere just a few years ago, rising up through the ranks like something I'd never seen.

"The fuck do you want."

He smiled, showing perfectly straight teeth. The fucker was a college boy, and he'd definitely seen an orthodontist or two. The guy might be covered in tats but something about him screamed rich suburbia.

How the hell someone like him ending up riding with someone like Dante was beyond me.

The rumor was, Shane was ass-balls crazy. Fearless. The man had apparently driven his bike off the roof of a drug store onto a big rig. He'd done the whole stunt on a dare.

I shook my head.

You'd have to be nuts to be that close to Dante.

"Shane."

"Mason."

"What do you want?"

He smiled and I felt my spine straighten. Someone had called him pretty boy once. I was pretty sure that guy was now missing a couple of fingers.

"Don't bother with the charm, you smug bastard. You Raisers are officially banned."

He held up his hands.

"I thought you'd like to know that the Hell Raisers are under new leadership. I'm here soley as a sign of respect."

"New leadership?"

He nodded slowly.

"Mine." He smiled again and I got a chill down my back. "Your little problem is solved."

I stopped with the bottle halfway to my lips.

"What little problem?"

He just smiled wider.

"Casey's safe from us. I don't care about her or that big fed of hers."

I set the beer down and stared at him.

"Where is Dante?"

"He won't be an issue. I can promise you that."

I got a chill. Dante was dead. I could see it in his eyes.

Man, this guy was crazier than I thought.

"Good to know."

He smiled and I felt like I was watching a commercial for cologne. Or imported beer. The man really was a little too good-looking.

"Oh and we will be back Mason." He winked. "There's no way I'm giving up that barbecue."

"I'll send you a bottle."

He laughed and walked out. I didn't much care for the man's arrogance. But I knew in my gut that things were going to be okay.

Besides, Shane might be nuts, but he wasn't a sick fuck like Dante. Casey was safe. Against all the odds, it was going to be okay.

I picked up the phone and called Connor again.

CONNOR

"Jesus Christ."

The body hung in the air, suspended from the normally busy bridge. Of course, now it was empty, other than every cop and federal agent in the county. The man was hanging there, strung up by the neck.

He swayed in the breeze like some sot of gruesome pinata.

After being burned, and then dragged, the body was almost unrecognizable. But the ride wasn't. I knew instantly who it was.

The bike that was crashed on the ground nearby was one hundred percent Dante.

Holy shit. Dante was really dead. The fucking bastard was worm food.

My phone beeped and I saw that Mason was calling me again. I sighed and rubbed my face. I decided I better take this.

Considering the man was going to be my de facto father-in-law I had to try and make nice. Or something-in-law. Anyway, we were about to be related.

So I answered.

"Hello."

"He's dead. He's fucking dead. You can bring her home now."

I didn't bother asking him who he was talking about, or how he knew. I leaned against my car and closed my eyes.

"News travels fast."

"You got confirmation?"

"I'm looking at it."

"Great. Bring her home."

"That's not going to happen, Mase."

"What the fuck man, you said you were protecting her!"

"What if the Raisers think you had something to do with it?"

He laughed and I knew without a doubt he knew who had killed Dante. I wondered if he'd been dead when they strung him up. I kind of doubted it.

Dante had pissed on a lot of boots over the years. The body looked worked over. Oh yeah, he had suffered.

A lot by the looks of it.

"Not an issue. *Bring. Her. Home.*"

"No."

"You doing something you shouldn't?"

I sighed and rubbed my eyes.

"I'm keeping her."

Total silence.

"The fuck you are! What the hell did you do, you cock sucker?"

Well Mason, I chained her up, fucked her six ways from Sunday and came down her throat. How's that for starters?

But I didn't say that. I wanted to live the rest of my life not looking over my damn shoulder. Mason wouldn't just kill me. I stared up at the body. He'd 'Dante' me.

"She's mine now. My responsibility. You can stop it with the mother hen act."

"No. She's my responsibility. And you are a dead man!"

"I'm marrying her Mase."

"What?"

His voice came out as a low growl. I wished I could see his face at the moment. On second thought-maybe not a brilliant idea.

"You heard me."

"Did she agree to that?"

I laughed. This was ridiculous. But... well, damn. She hadn't exactly said yes now, had she?

"More or less."

"You get her fanny over here, or on the phone, today. Or else."

I nodded. The man deserved to see her. But I had to make sure he didn't try and keep her.

"I'll bring her by with the pets."

"When?"

"Tonight."

Then I hung up and stared at the body gently swaying in the breeze. I had a fuck ton of work to do. And now I was even further from catching Danny's killer. Because if it was Dante, he'd never face trial.

But I was getting married. And my girl was safe.

I was the only person working the grisly crime scene that day with a shit eating grin on his face.

CASSANDRA

"Y ou look beautiful."

Connor kissed my neck as I stared in the bathroom window. I had picked out a few of the fancier things in the bags Conn had brought me. I was wearing a dark gray turtleneck dress made out of a soft, thick knit. It hugged my curves and brought out my eyes.

That's what Conn said anyway.

I tugged the skirt down to my knees, wondering if it was too much.

I was so nervous about seeing Mase. Now that things were different, I knew he might not approve of my relationship with Connor.

Conn was taking me home.

Except... this was my new home. Wasn't it?

"I do?"

He nodded, his hands sliding over me. "Yes. I wish we had more time so I could show you how beautiful." I laughed and turned in his arms to kiss him.

He growled and bit my lip, pushing me up against the wall. His fingers slid up under my skirt and he moaned.

"Did you forget your panties you naughty girl?"

I smiled.

"I thought I'd give you something to think about while we were out."

"Fuck... trust me, I don't need any help being distracted."

He pressed his cock against me to prove his point. I felt my skin get hot and cold just from the feel of him. Well, I guess he didn't need any distractions after all.

"I'll wear some if you want."

"Yeah, I do want. But first-"

He rubbed my pussy lips and stared at me as I gasped in pleasure. He circled my clit a few times and I moaned.

"What are you-"

"I'm getting you wet. If I'm going to suffer, then you are too." He grinned, pulling his finger away and slowly licking it clean "Besides, I want those panties back after."

My jaw dropped.

"You want me to get them- messy?"

He nodded slowly.

"I want them with me all day tomorrow."

I moaned as he winked and walked into the bedroom to get me a pair of panties. These were bright blue and soft cotton. I knew I was going to drip all over them.

I shimmied into my panties as Connor watched. He licked his lips and smiled. Then he took my hand and led me downstairs.

I stood on the porch with Besos and the cat case as Connor pulled the car up. He looked nice in a button down and jeans.

The man basically looked like a model for 'Studs R Us.'

I sighed and rubbed my legs together. He'd made me so horny upstairs... now I was going to have to wait all night until we were alone again.

He pulled the car up close and stared at me. The hunger in his gorgeous blue green eyes made me weak in the knees. He was as annoyed as I was that we had to wait.

Probably more.

He growled and kissed me hard, letting his hands roam under my skirt to check my panties.

Definitely more.

Well, they always said that misery loves company. So does extreme horniness apparently.

I helped him load the pets into the car. Con lifted the cats and I took Besos. Once everyone was inside he turned to me, checking my seatbelt, and caressing my nipples in the process. I moaned as a fresh wave of lust ran through me.

He smiled at me smugly and turned the ignition.

"Safety first."

I gave him a look, remembering his aversion to wearing condoms with me. "Ha, ha." But I was smiling the whole way to Mason's.

CONNOR

"Y"ou can let go of her now."

Mason smirked at me as he squeezed Casey so hard I was afraid he might hurt her. She hugged him back, her eyes a little misty.

I sighed, knowing my jealousy was irrational.

Still, I didn't like seeing someone else pawing my woman dammit!

"Okay now. Enough."

Casey giggled as Mason set her down.

"How the hell did you get so grown up, little girl?"

She shrugged and looked at me.

"I don't know."

Mason glared at me.

"You have some serious explaining to do, DeWitt."

He leaned over the pot of stew he was making and gave it a stir. It smelled fucking delicious. The man had a way with spices.

He grabbed a beer, not offering me one. I followed him into the living room. Casey brought me a cold one a minute later. I pulled her onto my lap and kissed her.

But just for a second. Because she was being lifted up and away from me.

"Hell no! Not on my watch! Hands off the goods!"

Mason had Casey's arm in a grip. She was smiling but I was worried he might bruise her. He was big and strong as an ox.

"Don't manhandle my future bride, Mason."

"I don't see a fucking ring on her finger. And I don't recall being asked for permission either!"

Casey rolled her eyes at us.

"I'm going to get myself a beer."

Mason let go of Casey as she slipped into the kitchen. I sat where I was. I knew if I stood up, Mase was going to take a swing at me.

I didn't want to have to beat the hell out of the guy who'd saved my woman from being a teenage runaway. Not to mention, he'd probably beat the hell out of me right back.

We were pretty well-matched, in terms of size and orneriness.

Not that I minded getting my hands dirty, or bloodied up for a good cause. I was itching for a fight. I had been ever since Danny died. But I didn't want to hurt Mason.

I owed the man.

"I'm not asking for your blessing. But I'd like it."
I cleared my throat. "I think Casey would like it."

He stared at me.

"Is this about getting your dick wet, DeWitt?
Because if you toss her aside I will come and rip out
your tonsils."

"Wow Mason, tonsils? That's so specific." We
both looked to see Casey standing in the doorway,
drinking her beer. "You are lucky, Conn. He
threatened to skin the last guy who asked me out."

"Do not get drunk-"

"Don't drink that too fast-"

Mason looked at me and we both realized how
ridiculous we were. There was almost a camaraderie
between us in that moment. But I was distracted by
what she'd just said.

"Who the hell asked you out?"

Casey shook her head and set her beer down.

"I'm taking Besos for a walk. Try not to kill each
other while I'm gone."

I was on my feet in an instant.

"A walk? By yourself?"

"It's fine. Dante's gone. I'm safe now. You told
me yourself."

Mason cleared his throat.

"Actually, Cain wants to see you, Casey. He's coming by."

I stared at him, my jaw ticking. Cain was the head of the Untouchables. Though some people treated Mason like he was a leader, he wasn't active in the gang. Cain was.

And the guy was fucking intense. Not as crazy as Dante or his second in command Shane. Cain was nowhere near as out of control. In fact, the man seemed to specialize in control.

The man ran his crew with military precision. He was cold and calculating. And he never, ever got caught.

Dante had been scary because he was a wild card.

Cain was scary because he was... not.

We both looked towards the door as we heard half a dozen roaring bikes pull up outside.

Fucking perfect.

CASSANDRA

I stared straight ahead, stopping now and then while Besos stopped to sniff something on the ground. I was doing my best not to be intimidated by the hulking, silent man beside me.

Not that I wasn't used to big men. Mason was a big guy. Connor was too. They were giants really.

But Cain was something else altogether.

He was big, but also quiet. Silent really. He saw everything that happened around him but he rarely said a word.

The head of Mason's former gang had never once said anything to me. All the times he'd been in The Jar, someone else had ordered for him. He was feared and worshipped by the bikers around here.

Not just the Untouchables either. Everyone.

And now he was escorting me around the block while my scruffy little dog peed on trashcans. *Still* not talking.

It was pretty much the weirdest ten minutes of my life.

A handful of the Untouchables were loitering in front of Mase's house while Cain and I took our little stroll. As we rounded the last corner he paused in his step.

When he stopped, I stopped.

He didn't look at me. And I didn't look at him.

"You didn't talk."

"No."

"And you won't."

"No."

He made a gruff sound of approval and strode the last ten feet to his bike. Without a word they all followed suit and tore off into the night. Connor and Mason came outside and looked at me.

I shrugged, holding up the plastic deli bag.

"He didn't feel like going."

Mason laughed and Connor ran his hands through his hair. He ran out to the sidewalk and pulled me into his arms.

"You alright?"

"Yeah. He didn't really say much."

"Mason said he was just making it known that he was cool with you."

"Oh." I nodded. "That makes sense."

"Mason said you were one of them now. Officially. That Cain's visit was a sign of respect."

I shrugged.

"I guess?"

He looked at me, swallowing hard.

"Case- I don't *want* you to be one of them."

I shrugged his arm off my shoulder. I was furious. After all of this- after everything- he was going to throw that superior good guy/bad guy crap in my face?

"If you aren't cool with who I am, or where I came from, then just say it."

"No- no, I didn't mean that. It's just- one of these guys. One of them-" He exhaled and stared at me. His eyes were full of raw pain. "One of them killed my partner."

I reached out for him, touching his chest.

"It was one of the Untouchables?"

"I don't think so. We were investigating the Raisers. But-"

I broke away. That was bullshit. He *was* looking down on me and Mase!

"But nothing. You can't lump all these guys in together. That's- well, it's wrong to judge people that way. Look at Mason and Dante. Do you think they are the same?"

"No. But I think they've both killed people."

Now it was my turn to look shocked.

"Mase- what?"

Conn shook his head.

"It's not my story to tell. But yeah. I think most of these guys are killers or capable of it. He's nothing like Dante. He's a good guy for the most part. But that doesn't change that we aren't on the same side."

He stared at me, his jaw ticking. I slumped, feeling suddenly tired.

"I just- I think I want to go inside now."

He pressed a kiss to my forehead and nodded.

"Yeah. We can talk about this later- at home."

CONNOR

"What do you mean she's not coming home with me?"

"This is her home. And until I see the two of you standing at the alter in front of a Goddamn preacher, that aint' gonna change."

"Casey! Get back in here!"

What the hell was happening? Why was she doing this? I shouted again but she didn't answer.

Casey had gone in the back and hadn't come out again. I tried to barge past Mason but he stopped me.

"Let me talk to her dammit!"

He just shook his head.

"You pissed her off dude. Or something. She needs time."

He smirked at me.

"And I expect a ring and marriage license before you get your filthy paws on her again."

I moaned staring past him to the dark hallway. I had pissed her off when I talked about Mase. Dammit! I had plans for her tonight.

And tomorrow morning.

And all weekend.

And the rest of our damn lives!

She was mine, dammit!

"I fucking knew I should have just let you talk on the phone."

He chuckled.

"Thanks for bringing the pets by. You took good care of them."

"Of course I did. Jesus!"

He walked me to the door as I dragged my feet, staring down the hallway. I kept hoping she'd peek her head out. Wave at me.

Come home with me.

At least give me those damn panties! I moaned, realizing how wet they must be from all the teasing I'd done... the soft blue cotton must be dark and sweet with her juices by now. I'd gotten her all riled up so we could suffer together.

Well, now I was the one in pain and there was no end in sight.

I was in a daze of confusion as Mason pushed me out the door and started to shut it.

"Wait-"

"Yeah?"

"I need to fucking talk to her!"

"She's got her phone back now, no thanks to you. She'll call you."

CASSANDRA

I curled on my bed, fighting back tears. Connor said he wanted to be with me, but he wasn't okay with who I was. Who my people were.

And that wasn't the worst of it. The worst was what he hadn't said. He'd never said the three little words that would have made this okay.

He'd never said 'I love you.' Maybe he *didn't* love me. I pressed my hands over my face as the tears fell.

I loved *him,* dammit!

Maybe this was all a mistake.

Had he tricked me without meaning to? Made me love him because I was confusing sex and love? I'd never been with anyone before. Never had much of a crush, other than on movie and television stars.

Not since grade school.

I was so stupid. He wanted someone else. Someone who wasn't a runaway who worked in a biker bar. I felt like my heart was ripping open as I realized that I wasn't that girl.

He wanted Cassandra Elliot.

The bright-eyed, straight A student who loved turning cartwheels in the backyard. I'd loved dancing more than anything, dreaming of making it a career.

That girl would have grown up. Gone to the prom. Had a boyfriend or two. Gone off to college.

That was a girl his mother would have been happy to meet. Not a scraggly waitress in a biker bar who didn't even have a real name anymore.

I was no one. In so many ways, I was invisible. I didn't count. Not to someone like *him*.

I rolled over, hugging my pillow to my chest. All the things he'd done to me. Maybe he just wanted that? Sex, without love.

Maybe he'd just been marrying me to protect me for a legal reason. Or because he was a control freak more like it. Did he just want a marriage of convenience?

And what he'd said about Mase… well, that was fucking my head up too.

Was my guardian, my savior, really a killer?

I knew he'd been wild in his day. He could give a beatdown like nobody's business. He had to in the bar, when the bouncers needed back up.

But a killer? I couldn't imagine the tough but gentle man who took in stray animals hurting someone out of spite.

Only to protect someone he cared about.

Maybe that's what Conn was talking about. Mason *would* kill someone who hurt one of his own, or even threatened to.

A soft knock at my door had me sitting up and wiping the tears from my face.

"You up?"

"Yes."

"You want to tell me what that was about?"

"Conn? I got mixed up with him. That's all. He didn't do anything wrong."

"Why'd you let him leave without talking to him then? If he hurt you-"

"No." I shook my head vigorously. "He didn't. He wouldn't."

I took a deep breath.

"He was upset about Cain."

Mase crossed his arms and leaned against the doorframe.

"Jealous?"

"No- he just- he doesn't want me to be part of this world. But I am. This is who I am. If he doesn't want that then... he doesn't want me."

"You're much more than this world, Case. You know that. You're going to get out." He sat on the edge of the bed. "College and then the world."

I shrugged.

"Maybe. But it doesn't change the fact of who I am now. And it still felt like he was... looking down on me." I lifted my eyes to his. "On *us*. In a way."

"Yeah, he's a pompous ass sometimes. But he has a good reason to hate bikers. His partner-"

"I know. But- he said that all bikers were killers." I looked at the gentle giant sitting at the foot of my bed. "Even you."

"Oh."

"Yeah."

He took a deep breath. Then he shook his head.

"It was a long time ago." I swallowed nervously and waited as he heaved a sigh. "You deserve to know, Case. It's not a short story though."

I leaned back and nodded.

"Okay."

"Connor's right. I have a record. Manslaughter charges that were brought and then dropped."

I exhaled, feeling the world tip upside down. Mason? A killer?

"Things were so different back then. The Untouchables were my family. I was one of them. *Just like them.* A lot of people expected me to take over someday."

He closed his eyes, tilting his head back against the wall.

"I was in charge of the new recruits. It was a testament of Sawyer's trust in me. Sawyer ran the Untouchables before Cain took over. Before Cain came back from Iraq, everyone thought it would be me. I was second in command. I wanted it. And then things got out of hand."

I pulled my knees up to my chest. I wasn't sure I wanted to hear the rest of this. I'd always known Mase had a past. I just didn't expect this- any of it.

It explained why the Untouchables and the Raisers treated him with so much respect though.

"You know how the new recruits are- they do anything and everything we ask. The guys push them- fuck with them- sometimes too hard." He ran his hands through his long brown hair. "But this kid, he had a condition or something. No one knew about it. I don't know if the kid- Pete- even knew."

He exhaled and covered his face.

"Such a fucking waste. They were hazing him and the other new recruits at the Blue Light. I was there but I wasn't paying attention. They were feeding him beer through a funnel. But they took it too far."

The Blue Light was another biker bar, much rougher than The Jar. I'd never been there and never planned to.

"All the other recruits puked or passed out. But Pete just- he fucking died. It was gruesome. His intestines burst."

"That's awful. But that wasn't your fault."

"It was. I was in charge. I tried Case, but it was too late." I could see the remorse in his dark eyes. "I took him to the hospital. I took the blame for feeding him the booze. He was just a fucking kid, barely old enough to drink. I should have protected him."

"Mase-"

"It was my fault Case. It was. Yeah, it's a dangerous life to ride with the Untouchables. But this wasn't anything like that. It was fucking frat boy shit. And I was in the back, fooling around with another man's wife."

My eyes got wide.

"You were-"

"I was busy getting my knob shined."

"Is that why you don't- go out with anyone?"

He laughed harshly.

"Yeah, I gave up women. It wasn't her fault, even though she was a pretty fucked up human being. I let her talk me into the affair, and I went in the back to get my rocks off."

He sighed and I wanted to hug him. But Mason didn't look like he wanted a hug right now, so I let him be.

"So yeah, I stopped chasing women. I couldn't enjoy it, knowing how bad I fucked up. I don't know if I even believe in love anyway."

My heart broke as he laughed bitterly and shook his head.

"But I know I don't deserve it."

CONNOR

"**A**nswer my damn calls!"

I hung up, swearing as I paced around the outside of the building. I was at work, trying to distract myself from the fact that Casey left me last night.

Left me.

And now she wasn't taking my calls or responding to my texts. I'd sent a dozen texts at least since leaving last night. I'd sat in my car, demanding that she come out. I'd called. Multiple times.

I'd slept with the damn phone on the pillow next to me! But nothing. And I'd barely gotten more than a few winks.

Mickey waved at me as he came out for a smoke but thankfully left me be. People were giving me a wide birth today.

Everyone knew the shark was back.

I was in a foul mood and wasn't being shy about it. Being up all night with a raging boner would do that to a guy. A raging boner with no relief in sight.

My woman had left me.

I was about to throw the phone across the parking lot when the text popped up. I exhaled sharply, staring down at my phone.

I need some time to think.

> *Think about what? You agreed to marry me. You belong at home with me dammit!*

A few minutes passed as I paced back and forth. I knew she wasn't a slow typist so I started to get mad. Worried.

Fucking scared.

You don't know me. You look down on people like me.

> *What? No I fucking don't Casey. I know you!*

You don't even know my name.

I stared at my phone, my breath coming fast. What the fuck was happening? Was this because of what I'd said about Cain- or Mason?

> *I don't care who you hang out with. I care about you. You're mine dammit!*

No answer.

I roared and stormed to my car. I'd done some paperwork already, going through the motions of the job. Dante's murder had created a fuckton of red tape. I didn't care. The rest of it was going to have to wait.

I was going to get my woman.

CASSANDRA

I set the phone down, determined to ignore it. The house needed a good scrubbing, and I needed to do my laundry.

And Mase thought it was safe for me to go back to work, if I wanted. He had a few new girls coming in to train anyway. We'd been planning to cut back my hours for a while, since I was applying to school.

Or I had been, before Dante murdered someone in front of me.

I guess, now that he was gone, college was back on the table... too bad I had no idea what to do about the *rest* of my life.

I tied my hair back in a bandana and got to work. The animals jostled me for attention as I turned up the music and started sweeping. I mopped after and finally got on my hands and knees to get any stubborn spots.

Cleaning was a blissfully mindless experience. And doing it made me feel like I was contributing. In foster care, I'd always resented the chores they heaped on us. But here, I relished it.

I was scrubbing the floor when I realized someone was standing directly behind me. I froze, my heart pounding in my chest.

My first thought was that it was not Mason. Mason wore enormous biker boots. Even with the music blasting I would have heard him.

Hell, the house shook a little when Mason walked in.

I would have *felt* him.

I gasped as I was lifted to my feet. Arms came around me and I relaxed. I knew who was holding me. Connor. It was Connor.

I heaved a sigh of relief as kisses rained down on my neck. He rubbed his rough cheek against me as his hands slid up and down my body, then up again to cup my breasts. He squeezed and fondled them and I felt a hot answering pulse in my belly.

"Connor!"

I turned in his arms and stopped short at the look in his stunning eyes. Conn was in bad shape. He looked like someone else. Someone who was in pain.

"Are you okay?"

The music was still blasting but I heard him. His voice was ragged and raw as he answered me. He held onto me for dear life.

"You left me."

I blinked.

"I didn't leave. I just needed some time to think."

"You left me." He exhaled and rested his forehead against mine. "Never do that again."

He lifted me up and carried me down the hall. He seemed to know which room was mine as he shoved the door open and lowered me to the bed.

"Conn-"

He started pulling his clothes off, shaking his head at me.

"Talk later."

I stared hungrily at his beautiful body as he stripped. He tried to take his pants off without removing his shoes. I giggled at the look on his face when he realized what he'd done.

He growled and kicked his shoes off. Then he pounced on me. The tiny bed shook as he covered me with his big naked body.

I'd been right. He *was* a panther.

He moaned in desperation as his fingers dragged down the front of my body.

"Open."

"We should talk-"

"After. Open your thighs."

I swallowed nervously and stared at him. He looked wild. He did not look capable of talking. I leaned back and let my legs slide open.

He growled at me.

"Wider."

I did as he asked then let out a yelp as he tore the crotch of my shorts wide open. They were old cut off jeans. The soft fabric tore easily under his strong hands. He dove down, his lips colliding with my panties.

A fresh pair. Not the blue ones that had been soaked when I went to bed last night. These were faded pink.

He cursed and tore those off too.

Well, not the whole way off. Just *open*. Enough for him to get at me.

I gasped as his tongue dove into me, no teasing this time. No slow build. He fucked me with his tongue for several minutes and then reared up, stroking his cock.

"Can't wait."

He pressed the hot, hard tip against me and fell forward, his weight pressing me down into the bed. My legs came up to wrap around him as he pushed his cock slowly inside me.

As soon as he was all the way in he paused, letting me adjust to his size. We stared at each other for a long moment. He kissed me hard.

Then he went wild.

His hips circled, never pulling out of me more than half way. He punished me with his cock, driving it in harder with each thrust. He didn't take his time. He picked up speed fast.

"I'm going to come."

I was close but not close enough. He must have known that because he reached down to strum my clit at the same time that he pulled my nipple into his mouth.

I screamed as the orgasm tore through me, taking me by surprise. I came hard. Almost *too* hard.

I'd been pretty pent up too.

Conn was grunting and cursing as he flexed his hips out of tempo, convulsing with the force of his orgasm. He shook above me, his hips jerking as I felt his seed hit the back of my womb.

"He didn't kill anyone! He took the blame for some other guys who were hazing a new recruit!"

We were still in bed, finally talking. Well, I was talking. Conn was kissing me, and touching me. I kept slapping his hands away but he was undeterred.

It was like he couldn't get enough of me.

Like he didn't believe I was real.

Or like he was terrified to lose me again.

"Are you even listening to me?"

He nodded, lowering his head to kiss my nipple.

"I believe you, Case."

His tongue lapped against my breast eagerly as he let his teeth slide over it. He was so fixated on my body, but it was more than that. I knew that now.

The moment I'd seen that raw look in his eyes, I knew.

Even if he didn't love-love me, he cared. This wasn't just sex. He needed me.

I took a deep breath. I had to tell him. It was time.

CONNOR

"My name's not Casey." She exhaled. "It's Cassie. Cassandra."

I stared at her, noticing a single tear spill from her gorgeous blue eyes. I brushed the tear away from her cheek. I smiled, feeling like I'd just won a prize.

The best prize.

"Cassandra. I like it."

I kissed her softly. She looked so worried. As if I might not like her real name.

"What is your last name?" I smiled tenderly. "I need it for the marriage license."

She sighed, chewing her lip. I wondered for the thousandth time what she'd been running from. Whatever it was, I would take care of it.

She never had to worry again.

"It's okay, if you are in trouble we can figure it out together."

"It's not that. It's just that- it's my parents' name." She let out a sad sigh. "And that little girl with a nice family doesn't exist anymore."

My heart broke a little, staring at her beautiful face. She was trying to be brave. But it killed me having to see her like this.

"We can get your name changed. You can be whoever you want." I grinned and pulled her closer. "As long as your last name is DeWitt."

She laughed breathlessly and nodded.

"Okay. My name was, it *is,* Cassandra Elliot."

I kissed her, so grateful that she'd finally given me her trust.

"It's beautiful. Just like you." I swallowed over the sudden lump in my throat. "I love you so much, Cassandra Elliot."

She stared up at me, her big eyes searching mine.

"You do?"

"Of course I do. Didn't I tell you that?"

"No. You didn't."

"Well, I'm a dumbass. I thought you knew how I felt Case- Cassie."

She blushed.

"No. I didn't. I thought-"

I pulled her closer, rubbing my cheek against hers. She sighed and I reached down between her thighs, gently toying with her slippery folds. I wanted her again, badly.

"You thought what?"

"Oh... hmmm... I thought- you just-"

I teased her clit and her hips rose.

"I just what…?"

"I thought you just wanted sex."

I stared at her, my hand still. Then she whimpered and I tapped her clit. Hard. She moaned and I decided that by the time I was done, she would know how I felt.

"Just sex?"

I increased the tempo of my finger. Rapid fire taps on her clit. She started panting, already on edge.

"I want much more than sex."

I was hard and desperate to get back inside her. I didn't hold back as I braced my body above hers and guided my fat cock to her perfect pussy.

"I want you in the morning. The middle of the night. I want you when you get old. When you are cranky. I want you to carry my child."

I thrust into her with each sentence. With each truth.

"I want you in sickness and in health. I want you when you are a pain in the ass. When you are sleepy. When you bounce around the room like a teenager."

"Ahhhh!"

She was coming. I smiled and continued my slow, hard thrusts, riding through the convulsions that massaged my cock so deliciously.

"I love you, Casey Cassandra Cassie Elliot Jones. I fucking love you."

I grimaced as my balls started to hum. I was close too. They rolled over, ready to explode.

"And yes, I plan on doing this as much as humanly fucking possible too."

Her back arched up as her orgasm continued, growing even stronger. My cock jerked inside her, spraying her with my seed. I tried to speak but I couldn't, my orgasm was way too intense.

"Ah! Fuck!"

I pounded her harder into the twin bed with the rickety frame. It banged against the wall as I rode her, taking what was mine.

Giving her what was hers.

Because I belonged to this one beautiful girl. Heart and soul. And my cock.

Especially my cock.

I held her as the tremors passed, unable to stop myself from kissing her soft skin. Her hair. Her nose.

She sighed contentedly as I rolled to the side, bringing her with me.

I felt so good. So right. She was mine. She wasn't leaving me. I didn't have to be afraid anymore.

And I had this crazy idea that we'd just made a baby.

CASSANDRA

"What do you mean you're not coming home with me?"

I crossed my arms, locked in a staring contest with the massive man looming over me. Connor might be big, but I wasn't intimidated.

I wasn't backing down.

"Mase is right! I shouldn't just move in with you- we just met!"

"You love me!"

I sighed. I hadn't said it yet. And now I had to watch my words because I had a feeling Connor was on the verge of abducting me. Mase would not be so forgiving a second time. He'd come after me.

With reinforcements.

And then all hell would break loose.

"If you meant what you said- about getting married…"

"Yes I fucking meant it!"

"Then we'll move in after that."

His eyes nearly bugged out of his head.

"Are you kidding? You want me to wait until we are married?"

I nodded. He looked like steam was about to come out of his head.

"That could take weeks!"

"We can still fool around-"

"Christ, Cassie! Sneaking in a little nookie when Mason isn't looking is not the same and you know it!"

I shrugged.

"I can't just be at your beck and call. I need to make plans- I was going to apply to college."

"You can do that at my place." He cleared his throat. "*Our* place."

"I have a job, you are kind of far from The Jar."

His jaw dropped and this time I *did* see steam come out of his ears.

"You are not setting foot in that place without me ever again!"

I raised my eyebrows.

"Oh, yes I am."

He stepped forward until we were almost chest to chest. Or chest to stomach. He was a couple of feet taller than me.

"Oh, no you are not."

"Don't be an ass Connor. I said we could still be together."

"Be together? When?"

"When I have time."

He moaned and yanked me against him.

"But I need you baby. I need this."

He kissed me deeply, letting his hands run all over me.

"I'll give you a BJ if you stop arguing."

His eyes got really, really big. So did his cock. I giggled and licked my lips, tilting my head to the side, leaning back in his arms.

"You will?"

"Uh huh. One BJ for every day you are patient."

The poor man looked like he was going to faint. He opened his mouth to speak then he shut it again. Then he opened it again.

"One BJ a day?"

I nodded.

"And other stuff too. But a guaranteed blow job, just for being patient."

He closed his eyes. Then he opened them and gave me a suspicious look.

"Starting now? And you'll marry me when it's all set?"

I smiled, reaching for his pants. Slowly, I lowered myself to my knees and undid his pants. He made a harsh sound of surrender and I knew I had won.

"Starting now."

I pulled his cock free and bit my lip. He was so big but so delicious. I loved the way the skin of his cock was so silky. I even loved the veins that popped out of it.

He was hard just for me and I loved it.

I pulled his cock into my mouth and started sucking.

"Cass- oh God."

His hands tangled in my hair. He wasn't forcing me down onto his cock, he was just encouraging me. Giving pleasure as he took it. I hummed and traced the edge of his tip with my tongue.

His hips jerked and he muttered something about getting religion.

I smiled to myself, cupping his balls as I started to take him deeper, moving my head rhythmically up and down on his long, thick shaft. I gripped the base, twisting my head to the side with each stroke.

He was gasping for breath, moaning incoherently, his hips flexing. Even though we'd had sex twice already it didn't take long for me to taste the first salty spurt of his come.

"Cass- I'm gonna-"

He howled as I sucked harder, pulling the seed from his cock as he held my head, pumping in and out of it. I relaxed my jaw, slurping and swallowing as jets of come filled my mouth.

I was still sucking when he dropped his hands, his body coming to a halt. I pulled the last few drops from him as he sighed, telling me what a good girl I was.

I helped him put his cock back into his pants, carefully zipping him back up. He seemed too dazed to do it himself. I smiled and stood up, sliding my arms around his waist.

Big strong arms held me close as he kissed the top of my head.

"Jesus woman."

I smiled into his chest, not surprised that he was quiet. I was surprised at what he said next though.

"I'll be back. Sit tight. It will take a few days to get the license and everything arranged." He chucked me under the chin. "We'll be hitched by Thursday."

He kissed my lips and winked, leaving me standing in the kitchen with a dumbfounded look on my face.

Did he say Thursday?

I heard his car start, still staring at the kitchen door. He was off and running.

Well, I guess the man knows what he wants.

I was smiling as I wiped up the soapy water and started on the sink.

Connor loved me. Cassandra Elliot and Casey Jones and every version of me in between.

He loved *me*.

CONNOR

"Did you pick something yet?"

"Conn, we just got here."

My sister was out with Cassie, getting her a wedding dress. I'd called ahead and told them to hide the price tags. I knew Cass would be squirrely about getting a fancy dress.

And I wanted my angel to have the best for the big day. My sweet, ridiculously sexy, best blowjob giver in the whole world, perfect little angel.

"Well, hurry up! Nothing too sexy but make sure-"

She laughed at me and hung up.

I stared at the phone scowling. Then I shrugged. We still had seven days until the wedding, if all went as planned. I'd hoped for sooner but even with my pull, it took a while to set things up.

Still, that was seven days worth of blowjobs... I groaned and pressed down on my cock. My little angel was torturing me today, texting me to describe how badly she wanted to suck my cock, and how she would do it.

I doubted I'd let her finish like she had yesterday. I wanted the full shebang. But man, the sight of her on her knees with her lips wrapped around my cock had been amazing.

When we were married I decided I'd have to make a similar deal. Maybe if I did the dishes... she'd kiss my dick.

I nodded to myself. Brilliant plan, Conn. Bribe the woman for sexual favors. But fair was fair.

After all, she'd bribed me into waiting.

I was doing everything I could but the wedding was still a week away. I was nose to the grindstone to bring it all together. I'd brought in reinforcements too.

Sheila was helping me get a marriage license. I'd gotten the rings. My mom was setting up the venue, while my sister worked on Cassie.

Cassandra.

I shook my head. I was still getting used to that. It suited her though. She'd been smart to pick a fake name that was similar to her own.

You could always tell by the way someone responded when you said their name.

My girl was clever. And then some.

I stared at my laptop, feeling a moment of hesitation. I'd been thinking about this all day. Once I got the wedding stuff rolling, I needed to track down her identity to get Cassie new paperwork. She hadn't been old enough to know her social.

All I had was a name and the town she was born in.

She'd been through so much. I didn't want to bother her with this too. I knew it would only bring up painful memories.

I exhaled and typed her name into the system, saying a little prayer.

It was almost instantaneous. A photo of a beautiful girl in industrial lighting. She looked so sad, so lost. But softer. Like the world had just started kicking the shit out of her.

This was the photo they must have taken during intake.

I closed my eyes and opened her file. More photos- these were from before she'd entered the system. A happy normal family. Her mom was beautiful, not surprisingly. And her dad was a big strong guy.

Damn, they looked so happy. Not rich or famous. Just… normal.

And then boom. They go out for date night and never come back. A semi on the highway had gone into a skid, taking their crappy little car with them. If they'd had a bigger car, if the road hadn't been slick, if the truck driver had driven just a little bit slower… they might have survived.

I read the report with tears in my eyes.

They'd been crushed, dying instantly.

Leaving their bright-eyed girl alone. No close relatives. No one to look after her except an elderly neighbor who was too frail for the job.

The state had taken over.

And they had done a fucking shitty job. I flipped through the pages, starting to see more and more evidence of her unhappiness. Cassie's attitude changed. Her grades dropped. She became a 'discipline case' at school and a surly, unresponsive preteen during home visits from the social workers.

Oh, and she moved foster homes a half a dozen times.

I read to the end and closed it out. I never wanted to read it again, though I knew I would. Over and over until I'd memorized it.

As if that would change the hell she'd been through.

I jotted down her social and got it to Sheila. Then I went outside for some fresh air.

My perfect, sweet girl was a survivor. She'd been unwanted and unloved. How someone could turn their back on that beautiful girl was beyond me. But she didn't have to worry about that anymore.

From now on, she always had a home.

She had me.

My phone buzzed and I exhaled in pleased surprise. I decided then and there to call it an early day. My sister had dropped Cass off, *with* a dress.

Bless Kelly's heart, she'd even mentioned that the big ass biker was leaving for The Jar. She even used those words. I grinned, shaking my head.

'Big Ass Biker.'

I drove over to Mason's house with a shit-eating grin on my face. Cass was available to me. She was home alone.

It was blowjob time.

CASSANDRA

"Come in."

I smiled shyly at Connor as I opened the door. The look of happiness and expectation in his eyes was overwhelming.

He looked eager. And he should. For the past few days I've been greeting him with a blowjob.

Once in his car when he took me to see the wedding venue. Twice here. And now he looked ready for another go.

It felt very brazen but also fun. And naughty. And he was very, very appreciative to me afterwards.

So appreciative I hadn't been allowed to finish since that first day. Instead he seemed to always end up tossing me over the nearest piece of furniture and burying his face between my legs. And then screwing me so hard the bed nearly broke the last time.

That was yesterday, and pretty similar to the day before that.

I tugged his waist band and he came in, looking like a bull ready to charge. I could swear I saw a little steam coming out of his nostrils.

He shut the door and leaned against it. Then he kissed me, his hands roaming everywhere. I pulled back and sank to my knees. His eyes flared with appreciation as I pulled his already stiff cock out and into the cool air.

He's always hard for me and I love it.

I taste him, all salty and sweet. Then I work my tongue up and down a bit, teasing him. Then I start to suck him, long and slow and deep.

"Oh sweetheart- oh Jesus, that feels so fucking good!"

I hummed a bit in response and his hips jerked. He grabbed my head and I realized he was close. Whoa. He might actually let me finish this time.

As much as I loved having sex with Conn, I loved making him come this way. Almost as much. I loved the power I felt and the sexy sounds he made as I worshipped his cock.

I picked up the pace, cupping his heavy balls with my hand.

And then the door opened.

Not far. Not with Connor leaned against it. But enough to knock me away from his cock.

Oh my God.

Mason was home.

Connor furiously tried to cover himself, cursing a blue streak in the process. Mason couldn't get the door open but he saw me jump up. I could tell instantly that he got the gist of what was happening.

"Oh hell no!"

Connor zipped his pants up and stepped away from the door. His jaw was ticking and I could tell he was beyond frustrated. But he looked cool as a cucumber.

A hard, unsatisfied cucumber.

"Out!"

Mason pointed at Conn and roared. I hid my smile with my hand. The two of them were like rams, ready to charge each other. I rolled my eyes.

It was a good thing the two of them had such incredibly thick skulls.

"I thought you were gone, Mase."

He gave me a look.

"Obviously." He glared at Conn again. "I forgot the sauce."

Mase made the base of his secret sauce here, then the cooks at The Jar mixed it with tomato paste and vinegar. It was his pride and joy, the recipe passed down from his grandma and improved on by Mase.

No one knew the recipe, not even me.

"You have a lot of nerve coming in here and taking advantage of her under my roof. *My* roof, DeWitt!"

"I'm not taking advantage of her! I'm marrying her for Christ's sake!"

"I don't see a ring on her finger, you fucker!"

My eyes got big as Connor pulled out a jewelry box. Wow. Talk about spoiling the moment.

"I have it right here! I- got distracted."

I stifled a laugh as Mason shook his head.

"Yeah you got fucking distracted. By your dick."

"I was going to propose!"

"Uh huh. I thought it was usually the guy who got on his knees."

Conn's mouth dropped open. What could he say to that? I turned bright pink.

Yeah, Mase knew exactly what we'd been up to.

He sighed and jerked his head towards the door.

"Get out of here."

"But-"

"No more visits until the wedding either!"

"That's seven days!"

"I don't give a fuck!"

"That's torture!"

"It's tradition! Now get the fuck out!"

I shrugged helplessly as Connor stormed out the door. He turned to stare at me.

"Cassie-"

I burst into laughter as Mason slammed the door in Conn's face. Mase grinned at me, locking the door.

"What? Was he going to propose with me here?"

I shook my head helplessly. I felt terrible for Conn but the look on his face was too funny. I knew he was going to be hurting tonight from that interrupted blowjob.

"Are you really going to make him wait all week to see me?"

Mason nodded.

"Trust me, he can handle it. The man has ice in his veins. You sure you want to marry him, Cass?"

Mason had started calling me Cass too. It was funny how much more I felt like myself. And it was all because of Conn.

"I'm sure. I love him."

"Love?" Mase sighed heavily. "Have you told him that yet?"

I shook my head and Mason grinned.

"Good. Nothing wrong with making a man suffer a bit for what he really wants."

I bit my lip as Mason hoisted the tub of sauce out of the fridge.

Well, Mase was right about one thing. Whether it was good or not, Conn was definitely going to suffer.

CONNOR

I stared at the ceiling. If I could sleep, the misery would stop. But I couldn't sleep in the condition I was in. No man could.

Seven days of hell.

It'd been a week. A week since I'd been alone with my woman. A week since her gorgeous lips had been wrapped around my cock, on the brink of milking me for everything I was worth.

I'd been in pain, suffering through an epic case of blue balls ever since. Every night, every damn minute, I was aching for her. Unsatisfied and unfulfilled.

But tomorrow all that would change.

Tomorrow, I was marrying her.

I glanced at the clock. Make that today. It was already after six and just starting to get light. I decided to make coffee and go for a run.

Anything to keep my mind off all the hours I had to wait. Or the man I had to thank for my heavy balls and heavy heart.

Oh yeah, payback for Mason was going to be a bitch.

Planning all the ways I would make his life difficult had become my second favorite thing to fantasize about this week.

I made coffee, staring around the house while I stretched. The food bowls were still out, clean and waiting. Maybe we'd get a pet. A shelter animal, like Mase had done.

Cass would like that I think.

It was so empty without her here. I'd always loved the peace and quiet. Craved the time by myself, with no one to bother me. I wanted to be left alone. But now I hated it.

It meant she was gone.

Well, she was coming home tonight dammit. Or after the weekend I'd booked us at a five-star hotel. And this time she was coming home for good. And if she ever left again, I *would* chain her to the damn wall.

I smiled as I remembered the only time I'd seen her beautiful face all week. Mason had allowed me one half hour with her, under supervision. I'd proposed, my cock aching and hard as I slid to my knees.

I'd asked her formally to become my wife. Cass had said yes with tears in her eyes and then I'd kissed her, taking my time and ignoring Mason completely.

Unfortunately, kissing her had only made me harder.

Yeah, I was dealing with a 24/7 megaboner. And it wasn't fun. But I could still work and I could still run, even if my fucking balls felt like lead weights!

I chugged a half a cup of coffee and hit the ground at full speed. It was cool and still kind of dark but I knew the trails around my house well. I was the one who had cleared them, widening the paths that the deer and other animals took. I'd connected several of them so they circled back towards the cabin.

I didn't need to do much of a warm up, not after the FBI had put me through my paces. The training had been brutal, and I'd done my best to keep up with it.

I did pushups and sit-ups every day. I ran. And I planned on having some very athletic sex over the next forty-eight hours.

What had Danny called it?

Sport sex.

I was going to have a lot of sport sex. I grinned as the sweat poured down my face, but it quickly faded. Danny would have loved Cass. He would have laughed his ass off at the hoops she was making me jump through.

I headed home and showered, staring at the dark grey suit I'd bought for the wedding. Kelly had gone with me, forcing me to class it up for this. All the way up.

The damn suit was expensive. But Cass was more than worth it. I wanted to look sharp for her.

I wanted everything to be perfect.

But as I shaved, I couldn't stop thinking about it.

Danny should have been my best man.

He should have been here with me.

I heard his voice in my mind, loud and clear and so familiar it made my heart ache.

I am, brother. Make me proud. Go get her.

He winked.

But don't do anything I wouldn't do.

I smiled and put on my suit.

CASSANDRA

"Who has a morning wedding anyway?"

Mase grumbled as he adjusted his tie. He looked so handsome in his suit. I knew he hated it, but he was doing it for me.

And I loved him for it.

"Where's your friend?"

I smirked, wondering how Mason would deal with Kelly and Mrs. DeWitt showing up here to do my hair. I shook my head.

"They are meeting me at the church."

I didn't know how he'd done it, but Conn had arranged for a wedding and a reception in just one week. Not just a tiny one either. There were almost two hundred people coming.

I was pretty sure it would be the first and last time the FBI and the Untouchables ever broke bread under one roof.

I smiled. What could go wrong? Conn had pulled it off though.

He'd said he would and he did. Maybe being a Special Agent had something to do with it.

Or maybe he was just the most determined human being on Earth. The most pent-up human being who was desperate to get his hands on me. Basically, he'd pulled out all the stops to get me in his bed.

Permanently.

Mason lifted the dress bag and walked me out to the limo Conn had sent. He'd grumbled something about not having me ride the back of Mason's bike with my damn wedding dress flapping in the breeze.

My car had mysteriously disappeared from The Jar, so I had no wheels. Conn had grinned when I mentioned it. Mase had said not to worry about it, but I knew the two of them were up to something.

I wasn't going to worry about that though. Not today. I was a bride today.

I was marrying the man I loved.

Of course, I wasn't sure I'd actually told him yet. But I would tonight. When we were in bed.

I giggled. Bed, or wherever else we ended up. I knew we probably wouldn't make it to the bed. Not the first time, anyway.

I practically skipped to the limo and climbed in, rolling down the window. I felt like a kid, excitedly bouncing in my seat. Mason rolled his eyes as I found a pop station and turned it up.

Way up.

He didn't say a word, even though I knew he hated it.

He was a good man. And he'd stood up for me with Conn, which meant so much to me. He'd even told me the truth about his past. I was lucky. For the first time since the accident, I really felt like I truly had a home.

Two homes actually.

I closed my eyes and let the breeze wash over me. It was sunny and warm for this time of year. A perfect day.

And I was getting married.

CONNOR

I *was getting married.*

I hoped so anyway. I paced back and forth at the front of the church, suddenly nervous. Mickey stood beside me, looking amused. Sheila sat in the front row with my mom, whispering in her ear and smirking at me.

Everyone thought I was nervous about getting married.

But they were wrong.

Tying myself to Cassandra for the rest of my life was the last thing I was worried about. I wasn't even bothered by the hundred tattoo covered guys who were sitting on the bride's side of the aisle, making my mother look like she might faint.

Oh yeah. Cass might be an orphan, but she had people now. Biker people. And I was just going to have to deal with it.

If they loved her half as much as I did, they couldn't be half bad.

I grimaced, pulling at my tie.

None of that was why I was sweating or had such a sour feeling in my stomach. No. I was just afraid the bride might not show up!

My sister appeared in the doorway and gave me a thumbs up. I felt all the tension leave my body. Cass was here. Now I just had to get her ass down the aisle!

I would not be relaxed until she'd said yes, and she was under me in that hotel room, screaming my name!

Hell, I might not relax until we were eighty!

The music started and I stood up straight, eager to get the show on the road. Everyone turned to look as Cass appeared in the doorway on Mason's arm.

She... looked... different...

My jaw dropped and my heart raced as I looked at my bride. I'd barely seen her in a dress even once. But this was something else.

Her natural beauty was dialed up to a gazillion. Her beautiful hair was pinned back with a delicate lace veil trailing over her shoulders.

Her bare shoulders.

Hot lust sliced through me. *Great, Conn. Real nice.* Now was not the time to get a fucking boner.

My angel's beautiful face looked so pure and perfect. She was done up just a bit, the subtle makeup enhancing those insanely gorgeous blue eyes of hers, and deepening the pink of her lips and cheeks.

The strapless dress hugged her curves, showing off those high, firm tits of hers. Um, breasts. I shouldn't call my wife's perfect jugs 'tits' right?

Not in church anyway.

I was pretty much drooling as she walked down the aisle. I continued staring at her in awe as Mason placed her hand in mine. The Preacher cleared his throat and I finally tore my eyes away from her.

Half the guys in the audience laughed.

Fuckers.

Oops, another bad word to be thinking during my wedding ceremony. I forced myself to focus on what the Preacher was saying, stealing glances at Cass the whole time.

She used her real name for the ceremony, which made my chest swell with pride. Then it was time for the 'I dos.'

I said mine so loud the entire crowd laughed this time. Even Cass turned pink. Her voice was soft but sure as she agreed to become my lawfully wedded wife.

"I, Cassandra Elliot, take you, Connor DeWitt, to be my husband, to have and to hold from this day forward, for better or for worse, for richer, for poorer, in sickness and in health. To love and to cherish from this day forward until death do us part."

I grinned as I slid the ring onto her finger. I melted like putty at the sweet, serious look in her stunning eyes as she slid a plain gold band onto mine.

"I now pronounce you man and wife."

And just like that. She was mine.

Mine. Mine mine mine!

"You may kiss the bride."

The crowd went wild as I pulled her against me, tipping her chin up. Then I kissed her, hard and long and deep. I lifted her off the ground, holding her against my rigid erection as I plundered her mouth with my tongue.

Cass was bright pink when I finally set her down on her feet again. Mase was glaring at me. I winked at him as I took off down the aisle, practically dragging my wife behind me.

I wanted to get to the limo. I wanted a quickie on the way to the party. I wanted her, now, dammit.

But the crowd rushed forward to congratulate us and we were stuck. The wedding photographer waylaid us and snapped about a thousand pictures on the church stairs.

We got couple photos, photos of the family, photos with Mason. A photo of me and my crew, with

Sheila front and center. Even a photo of Cass surrounded by the Untouchables.

It was almost an hour later when I was finally able to pull her away. I was grinning as I guided her into the limo and told the driver to take the scenic route. I took one last look at the crowd and froze, one foot inside the limo.

I saw something that made my blood run cold.

Cain was there. The head of the whole damn gang. And he was staring at my sister. And she was staring back at him.

Hell, Kelly was *smiling* at the giant brute.

I decided I needed to have a little talk with my sister about appropriate men when we got to the party.

But first, I had some pipe to lay.

CASSANDRA

"Come here wife."

Connor's eyes were dark as he pulled me against him for a kiss. His tongue delved deep into my mouth, tasting me with a growl.

I gasped as I felt his hands on my thighs. He had pushed my dress up to my waist.

"Conn!"

His lips found my neck and I felt my veil start to slip.

"What are you-"

"Lean back."

I stared at him as he guided me onto the limo seat and started tugging my panties down.

"You must be joking."

"Nuh uh."

I couldn't resist the boyish grin on his face. I sighed as he teased my pussy with his lips and tongue, tracing my sensitive nub with the lightest pressure. I felt myself responding and moaned.

He told me he loved me as he slipped a finger inside me. I arched my back as he worked his magic on my clit. I felt utterly depraved letting him eat me out like this in our wedding limo.

I was wearing white for goodness sake!

But he took his time, working me over with expert skill. The man knew what he was doing, and he was damned good at it.

I was a very lucky lady.

I decided Connor's secret superhero name should be Motor Tongue. Because the man was pretty much a machine. I screamed as I came, my body nearly sliding off the slippery leather seats.

Conn didn't stop though. He slid a second finger inside me and sucked my clit into his mouth. He flicked his tongue on me again.

Hard.

The world exploded. I saw stars as I came again, even harder. One orgasm on top of the other. It was too much. I faded out of consciousness.

When I came to, Conn was leaning over me, his eyes full of worry. He rubbed my hands, blowing on them.

"You okay, sweetheart? Jesus, you scared me."

"What happened?"

"I think you fainted."

I sat up slowly, looking around. The limo was stopped. I realized I still wasn't wearing panties.

"Where are my panties Conn?"

He grinned and patted his jacket.

"Finders keepers."

"Did we…?"

He shook his head.

"Uh, no things went off plan when you passed out. I think we need to get a doctor."

"I'm fine. I just-"

I covered my mouth as nausea overtook me.

"What is it?"

I lunged for the door and opened it. Just in time to vomit all over the parking lot.

"Oh my GOD!"

"Jesus, Cass! Are you alright?"

I sat back into the limo, praying that no one had seen me. I nodded, feeling immediately better. It felt like I'd never been nauseous to begin with.

I took the bottle of water he handed me and washed my mouth out twice before taking a long sip.

"Let's get you some food. No drinking tonight!"

"Yes, husband."

He grinned at me suddenly, but his eyes still looked worried.

"Say that again."

"Yes, husband. I love you, husband."

He beamed at me and scooped me up.

"I love you, wife."

He carried me inside the restaurant. People cheered as we came in but Mason was by my side in an instant.

"What's wrong with her?"

"She threw up. And fainted."

"She needs a doctor right now."

Sheila came over, looking concerned.

"What happened?" Conn told her and she looked at me, then back at Conn. "Sure she isn't pregnant?"

My jaw dropped. Conn's face turned white. And Mason started to literally give off steam.

"WHAT?" Conn set me in a chair and Mason grabbed him, twisting his shirt in his fist. "You couldn't use protection, you animal?"

Conn held up his hands. "I knew I was marrying her, Mason. There's no need to-" Mason yanked Conn closer and raised his fist.

"Mason!"

He stared at Connor, not throwing the punch but not lowering his fist either.

"You are very fucking lucky this is your wedding day."

Then he dropped his fist and walked away. Conn smiled at me, looking totally fine. Like he hadn't almost gotten beat to a pulp.

Like I wasn't possibly pregnant!

"How are you sweetie?"

"How am I?"

I must have looked incredulous because he laughed.

"Come on, I want to give you your wedding gift. It's from the two of us."

"Who?"

"Me and Mason of course. Can't you tell we are best friends now?"

My mouth opened in surprise. I felt like a jerk. I hadn't gotten him anything in return.

"I didn't get you a gift!"

He lifted me up again and kissed me.

"Sweetheart, you *are* the gift. And whether or not you are pregnant, I'm the luckiest son of a bitch in the world."

I snuggled against his chest as he carried me outside. Then I saw it. A shiny black SUV with a giant pink bow on it.

Mason was leaning on it, a wry grin on his face.

"Oh my God. You got me a car?"

"I bought it. Mason souped it up."

He set me down long enough for me to put my arms around Mason. He squeezed me back. Mase really loved me like a sister I realized, with tears in my eyes.

It was hard for Mase to show affection, but he showed it to me. I saw in his eyes. And that meant the world to me.

"Thank you so much." I lifted my eyes to Conn. "Thank you both."

Mason shrugged.

"It's not souped to go fast. It's got a nice sound system and extra safety features. Emergency break assist, lane departure warning and a roll bar." He smirked. "And an embedded tracking device."

I stared at the two of them. Tracking? Mase jerked his thumb at my husband.

"All him kid. Not a bad idea though."

"Connor!"

"I want to know where you are." He gave me a dark look. *"All the time."*

"You are twisted."

He shrugged sheepishly and scooped me up again.

"I worry about you sweetie, that's all."

I sighed and shook my head. He was so protective of me. I guess I was going to have to get used to it.

"Come on, there are a lot of people inside who want to see you." He scowled a little. "And I need to have a serious talk with Kelly."

CONNOR

I stared at my sleeping bride.

No, she was my wife. On paper and in our hearts. It was done.

At long last, Cass was my wife.

She'd been a trooper tonight, talking and chatting with all the guests. Dancing our first dance. She'd even gotten bossy, dragging me away from Kelly when my little sister looked like she might slug me.

I frowned.

Kelly had listened to me I think. I hadn't seen her near the big biker all night. But he made no effort to hide the fact that he was watching her.

Not just watching her. The man who never had a facial expression in his life was clearly lusting after my innocent little sister, who was 1000 percent off limit!

Great, just what I needed. Another fucking biker! And this one was after my little sister!

I grumbled, suddenly realizing how Mase had felt. Kelly was twenty-one and old enough to date. But I wasn't ready for it.

And I certainly wasn't going to allow her to be carried away by a badass biker!

Cass rolled over and mumbled in her sleep. We'd made love very carefully. And only once.

I was still pent up but there was a little something on the bedside table that kept me from waking her.

A pregnancy test.

We'd stopped at a twenty-four hours pharmacy on the way to the hotel. She'd waited in the limo as I ran inside. Then we'd come back and celebrated together by making the bed bounce.

She'd taken the test after we made love. Then she immediately fell asleep.

So I was alone, and staring at the damn thing.

The damn thing with the little blue plus sign on it.

My angel was pregnant.

I put my hands behind my head and grinned, feeling pleased with my manly prowess. I'd done that in record time! She couldn't be more than four weeks along, even if I knocked her up the first time we did it!

Come to think of it, that was probably exactly what had happened.

Cass snuggled up to me. I rolled to my side and kissed her shoulder. Her beautiful eyes opened, blinking at me like a little bird.

"What- time is it?"

"Just after one."

I kissed her bare shoulder, letting my hands run down her flank. I tried to imagine her with her belly rounded, and her perfect breasts growing big and ready to make milk.

"Conn?"

"Hmmm?"

"Why are you smiling like that?"

I rolled her to her back and kissed her, rubbing my cock against her sweetness.

"I'm a lucky bastard that's all."

"Why?"

"Because I'm married to you." I smiled at the shy look on her face. "And because I'm going to be a daddy."

Her eyes widened and she sat up, shoving me off her. I was caught between a moan and a laugh as my plans to take her again were interrupted. She grabbed the test and stared at it.

"Oh my God!"

I wrapped my arms around her, pulling her back to the pillows.

"We'll get a doctor appointment tomorrow. Just relax and let Daddy take care of you tonight." I smiled. "I'll always take care of you."

She slid her arms around my neck and wrapped one thigh over my hip in a blatant invitation.

"Alright, it's a deal. As long as…"

"What is it love?" I kissed her neck. "Anything you want."

"Stop calling yourself 'Daddy!'"

My laugh turned into a moan as my cock slipped just inside her. She was so wet and ready. And I was always ready.

We spent the weekend making love and napping. We made a list of doctors to call come Monday and even walked to a bookstore in town and bought a baby book.

It was the best weekend of my life.

And I knew it was just the start of it.

Yeah, I was one hell of a lucky bastard.

SEVEN AND A HALF MONTHS LATER

CONNER

I paced back and forth, running my hands through my hair. My angel was in labor and I was about to lose my ever-lovin' mind. The nurse was examining her, telling her it would be time soon.

Cass was fully dilated. I could hardly believe it. My wife was having our baby!

One of many, I hoped. I wanted a whole house full of adorable little Cassies and Connors. The more the merrier. I just hadn't told her that yet.

I knew she wanted to get through college first.

What a difference a year could bring. A year ago, I was alone and bitter. I had no love in my life, other than my mother and sister. I knew I'd been lucky to have Sheil and some of the guys too.

But I held everyone at bay. I shut them out. Without Danny, life had lost its luster.

I was still tracking his killer. All signs pointed to the Hell Raisers and not the Untouchables, thank God.

I think my wife would have my head if I messed with her extended family. Who were now *my* extended family too. I was starting to get used to them, in small doses. I even rode my vintage Indian with Mase now and then.

Wasn't that a kick in the pants?

She let out a groan and I raced across the room, taking her hand in mine.

"Are you okay?" She nodded and smiled weakly. I squeezed her hand and kissed the back of it. "I wish I could do this part for you sweetheart."

She laughed and then grimaced, as another contraction came on suddenly.

"I wish you could too."

I kissed her as the doctor came in. Everyone went into motion suddenly, the room a hive of activity. I held her hand as she pushed when told to, and helped her do her breathing exercises in between.

She stared at me between contractions, those bright blue piercing right through to my soul. I stood there, hiding my fear. I had to be strong for her, even if I was crying inside.

My angel had a way of bringing out the best in me. She didn't have to nag or wheedle. I just wanted to please her.

And I didn't mind impressing her now and then too.

It might make some men feel weak to know that they had a very visible chink in their armor. But it made me feel strong. I only had one real weakness, and that was her.

And whoever we were about to meet.

We had decided not to find out the sex in advance, decorating the nursery at the cabin in soft green and cream. Everything was ready for him or her. Cass was the one who had to do the hard part now.

Hours passed and Cassie started to lose her strength. The doctors told me not to worry, but I saw them exchange glances. I pulled them out into the hallway, hating leaving her for even a second.

"Is something wrong?"

"The baby is doing well, but Cassie's blood pressure is low. We need to get food and fluids into her."

She wrinkled her nose and moaned as another contraction hit. I ran back into the room. I knew the last thing she wanted was to eat. But she nodded when I told her.

I helped her sit up and fed her a couple of greasy fries and some juice. She loved fast food so getting the first few fries down was not hard. The salt was good for her too.

She waved me off after a few bites though. We sat there, waiting. When the next contraction hit she pushed. The doctor guided the baby out a few minutes later and we all heaved a sigh of relief. They cleaned the baby up and handed her to me.

We had a beautiful, perfect baby girl. I was filled with such pride, I could hardly believe what we had done. Together.

I carried her over to Cassie and froze, panic freezing me to the spot.

My angel was unconscious.

CASSANDRA

I moaned, trying to get away from the light. It was too bright, and hurting my eyes. I was cold and uncomfortable. And it hurt like the devil between my legs.

"Cassie, can you hear me? Mrs. DeWitt!"

I opened my eyes and blinked. A doctor was leaning over me, shining a flashlight into my eyes. Connor stood off to the side, his eyes glued to my face.

Connor looked like he'd seen a ghost. The man was *white*.

"Pupillary response looks good. We're going to need to keep her here a few days. Stabilize that BP."

Connor stared at me, his eyes full of pain. I'd never seen him look so afraid.

"Conn?"

"It's okay sweetie. You're okay."

"Where's the baby? Is it-"

"She's okay. Our beautiful daughter is fine."

The nurse came over and showed me our child. I lit up, my smile beaming as I reached for her. I still felt weak so Conn helped me support her in my arms.

"She's so beautiful."

He kissed my cheek.

"Just like her mama."

We sat there for the longest time before they came to take me for some tests. I was so tired, I kept falling asleep. Every time I woke up, though, Conn was by my side.

"Let me see her."

I sat up, realizing I must have passed out again. Mason stood in the doorway, looking livid. Conn was blocking his path, telling him it wasn't a good time.

"Let him in."

Mase strode across the room to loom over me. He squinted his eyes at me, looking me up and down.

"You okay, kid?"

"They said she's fine. They said it's-"

Mase turned and pointed his finger at Conn.

"You shut up. This is all your fault." He turned back to me. "That bad man shouldn't have done this to you."

I laughed. Mason never let Connor live it down that he'd knocked me up so soon in our relationship.

"I was a willing participant."

"I know, kid." He winked at me. "Where's the spawn?"

Conn asked a nurse to bring the baby back in. We'd named her Daniella, after Conn's partner. It had been my idea, and Conn's gorgeous eyes had made water when I brought it up.

The man had legit cried.

It was so sweet I swear I fell in love with Connor him all over again.

"This is Daniella. Daniella, this is your uncle Mason."

I handed the baby to Mason and he took her, holding her in his massive leather clad arms. He bounced her very softly, like she was the most precious thing in the world.

And to the three people in this room, plus a handful of others, she was.

"I was hoping you'd be her Godfather."

Mase stared at me, then back at our little girl. Conn shook his head and rolled his eyes. This part he hadn't argued with.

Even though I was pretty sure he'd wanted to.

Mase cleared his throat.

"You sure, kid? You know what kind of guy I am."

"Yeah." I smiled and reached out to put my hand on his leather clad arm. "The best guy."

Conn cleared his throat and I rolled my eyes.

"One of the *two* best guys." I clarified. My husband smiled goofily at me. He needed to hear how much I loved him as often as possible. I never minded telling him.

Mase laughed and put his big hand under Daniella's tiny feet.

"It would be my honor."

STOP!

P lease do NOT go back to the beginning of this book before closing it. If you do, the book will not count as being read and the author will not be credited.

Please use the TOC (located in the upper left hand of your screen) to navigate this book. If you're zoomed out, please tap the center of the screen to ensure you are out of page flip mode.

This is true for all authors enrolled in Kindle Unlimited and as such, this message will appear in all of our books that are enrolled in Kindle Unlimited.

Thank you so much for understanding,

Pincushion Press

ABOUT THE AUTHOR

Thank you for reading *Cuffed*! If you enjoyed this book please let me know on by reviewing and on and Goodreads! You can find me on Facebook, Twitter, or you can email me at: JoannaBlakeRomance@gmail.com

Sign up for my newsletter!

Credits:

LJ Anderson, Mayhem Cover Design

Furious Fotog, Cover Photo

Jordan Wheeler, Cover Model

Just One More Page Book Promotions

Pincushion Press

Other works by Joanna Blake:

Wanted By The Devil (Devil's Riders MC Club)

Still Waters (Devil's Riders MC Club)

Safe In His Arms (Devil's Riders MC Club)

Devil's Riders: Before You (A short prequel to the Devil's Rider's Trilogy)

Slay Me (Rock Gods)

Dare Me (Rock Gods)

Cover Me (Rock Gods)

BRO'

A Bad Boy For Summer

PLAYER

COMING SOON: The Continuation of Mason and Cain's stories in *The Untouchable's Trilogy*

Turn the page for excerpts from Joanna Blake's *Cockpit, GRIND, BRO'* and *A Bad Boy For Summer.*

COCKPIT

I rubbed my cheek where she'd slapped it, admiring the way she looked in those tight jeans of hers as she stomped off. She was a redhead alright. Only a russet haired woman would slap a man after kissing the hell out of him.

And Jenny was one hell of a kisser.

I took my time coming back in. Not because I was worried she'd slap me again. I was just deep in thought.

Mostly thinking about gettin' deep in her.

I sat down and ordered a watered down pitcher of beer. I had a long night ahead of me. I had someone to walk home.

Jenny scowled at me while she took my order, and scowled when she watched the other bartender bring it back. She scowled when she brought me a basket of fries.

The woman basically scowled up and down the whole night.

I sat back and waited for her shift to end, enjoying the memory of the way her luscious body had melted against me. It was getting close to time when she asked me if I wanted anything else. I took my time, staring up and down her body.

"Oh yeah honey, I can think of a lot of things."

"I'm not a piece of meat, Jagger!"

"No, you're definitely not a piece of meat. But you do look tender."

Jenny threw my check at me and turned tail to see to her other tables. I made my last beer count, sipping it slow as molasses until I was the last guy in the place. She started getting ready to close up. She 'accidentally' mopped right over my boots.

I smiled and stood up, throwing a fifty-dollar tip on the table. Her eyes widened. She stared at me as I walked out of the bar.

'Course I was waiting out front for her when she came out fifteen minutes later.

She stared at me. I stared at her. Then she walked up to me and tossed that fifty-dollar bill in my face.

"I'm not for sale you sonofabitch!"

I looked right at her. She was angry. But she had mistaken my meaning.

"I didn't say you were."

"Then what are you doing tipping like that?"

"I took up a seat in your section all night. Seemed fair."

She stared at me belligerently.

"Well, I'm not taking it."

"How about a twenty?"

"What are you, a cash machine?"

She huffed, crossing her arms over her chest. Her glorious, perfect, mind-bending chest. I pulled out a ten and a five.

"Fifteen?"

She yanked the money out of my hand so fast I got rug burn. Then she stomped off. The woman had a pair of legs on her. And she made good use of them.

I was whistling as I followed her back towards the base.

GRIND

Something wet slid against my ear. I brushed it away, still half asleep. It grazed my skin again and I rolled away from it. I tried to wipe it off on the pillow beneath my head, grimacing at the slimy sensation. Now I was awake and I didn't want to be.

Damn.

I opened my eyes to see a woman bending over me. Her long blond hair brushed my face. I turned my head away.

"Cut it out."

She sat up, glaring at me.

"You didn't seem to mind last night."

Normally, I would have soothed her. Called her by name. Trouble is, I had no fucking clue who the hell she was.

I looked around.

I had no idea where I was either.

"Fuck me."

She grinned at me, tossing that long bleached hair over her shoulder.

"I already did."

Belatedly I noticed that she was wearing some serious lingerie. Black and cream lace. It matched her bedroom. Her very expensive looking bedroom.

I was swimming in a sea of neutral toned sheets and blankets. Silk probably. Expensive, definitely.

"I'd like to again."

I shook my head.

"Sorry babe, I gotta go."

She pouted. I rolled out of bed, looking for my clothes.

"Oh come on... Didn't we have fun together last night?"

I smiled and nodded. It's not that she was bad looking, even if she was at least a decade older than me. It was hard to tell with these rich older broads. She was toned, buffed and polished to a high shine.

Well preserved didn't even begin to cover it.

Yeah, she was hot. Not just for a cougar. But I wasn't in the mood. I didn't usually go for seconds anyway.

Hell. I never did.

Hit it and quit it was my motto. It served me well. I didn't want any entanglements and I doubted I ever would.

I looked at her, giving my best impersonation of someone who gave a shit.

"Where are my clothes?"

She smiled back and shrugged.

"I really couldn't say."

<u>Fucking hell.</u>

"That's great. Just great."

I looked around the room, lifting cushions and opening drawers. Nada. On the bedside table were my keys, wallet and phone. I scooped them up, thanking God for small favors.

"Have a nice day, Ma'am."

"Wait- you aren't leaving like that!"

I coyly waved bye bye to her and left. I jogged through her palatial house in the buff. The marble floors were cool under my feet. The place screamed mega bucks. But not in a tacky way. It was tastefully done, just like the lady herself.

She was chasing me through the house, becoming less composed by the second.

"Seriously, you can't! What will the neighbors think?"

I stopped at the front door of her mansion, glancing back over my shoulder.

"You should have thought of that before you hid my shit."

She screamed in frustration and threw a vase at me. I heard it shatter against the door as I closed it behind me. Just in the nick of time.

"Damn. That would have left a mark."

I made a call as I strolled down her manicured driveway to the gate.

"Joss, can you pick me up? I need a ride."

I leaned against the wrought iron gate and waved at a neighbor who was walking their dog.

"Take your time."

BRO'

Not one for slacking I started my first full day home with a match against the club pro Matt. It cost extra to play with him but I didn't care. He was an amazing player and gave as good as he got. And for some reason, he considered me a friend.

Probably because most of the people who hired him were bored housewives hoping to get into his pants.

I'd noticed the cougar crowd dropping me hints the past few years as well. And now that I was 21... well maybe I'd take one of them up on it. At least I could be sure an older woman would know what she was doing.

I was dripping with sweat by the time we were done. I wasn't a big fan of showering at the club so I left. Matt waved me off and begged me to book him as much as possible this summer. I promised I would.

What the fuck else was I supposed to do?

Except, well, <u>fuck.</u>

As much as possible.

As many girls as possible.

Speaking of which maybe I'd text Jen later. I knew she was waiting on me. I did enjoy working out horizontally, especially with a sexy female like Jen. She liked to sport fuck as much as I did.

I was turning down our driveway in my convertible when I hit the breaks.

Hard.

A girl was biking toward me. From the general direction of the house. Long dark blond hair blew behind. Big high tits filled out her t-shirt admirably. She had a teeny tiny waist and long tanned legs. She rode closer and I tried to get a look at her face.

Pretty, that much was obvious, with big beautiful eyes. I could see her puffy lips from twenty feet away. Cute little nose too.

The girl looked like a God damned swimsuit model.

No. Wait. What.

My brain went utterly blank as I realized something.

It was Mouse. Mouse was the swim suit model. I was staring at Mouse with lust.

Hot, unrelenting lust.

I jolted to action as she pulled up by my car.

"Nev?"

She stopped her bike, those impossibly long legs straddling the seat. Her jean shorts were short, almost up to the top of her perfect thighs. I swallowed, realizing my mouth was a little bit dry.

But my dick was throbbing.

She smiled at me, cool as a cucumber. Where was the worshipful little Mouse I knew and loved?

"Hey Clay."

She'd grown up obviously. And she'd grown up right.

Still, I knew how to charm the pants off a girl, no matter how hot she was. And I wanted to. I knew it instantly. I wanted to fuck Mouse, of all people.

Really, really bad.

I smiled, letting my eyes wander over that ridiculously perfect little body.

"Where you going?"

She tossed her head, sending a cascade of wavy blond hair over her shoulder. It was very sexy, but not deliberate or coy. She was unconsciously seductive. It was hypnotizing.

"Job hunting."

I smirked.

"In that outfit?"

She looked down at herself and back at me.

I pulled my sunglasses down and switched gears.

"I think you've outgrown those shorts little Mouse."

Then I drove away. Slowly. Very slowly.

Just so I could check out her ass in the rear view window.

Good lord, the girl was fine. She'd stop traffic anywhere. No matter what she was wearing.

I went into the house to change, all thoughts of texting Jen forgotten.

A BAD BOY FOR SUMMER

I threw my arm over the back of the seat and looked to the side, letting my eyes slide over her body. Frannie didn't seem to notice. Her hands were gripping the bar that had locked us into place in the Ferris wheel seat.

I leaned back and watched her as the ride started to spin.

She looked like a little kid, nervous and excited. Her cheeks were pink and her eyes sparkled when she turned to look at me.

"I thought you didn't like Ferris wheels."

"I don't! I'm petrified."

I grinned at her.

"I'll protect you."

She laughed as if that were the wittiest thing I could have said. I laughed too, her laughter was that infectious. As soon as we got to the top of the wheel I slid over to her. Her face was startled as she looked into my eyes. My eyes lowered to her soft inviting lips.

I leaned in and tilted my head, angling my mouth against hers.

Her lips felt like pillows underneath mine. Warm and sweet. Her breath mingled with mine as I slowly eased into the kiss, nibbling and licking her until she opened her mouth.

Then the kiss went wild.

My hands reached for her hips as I pulled her against me. Her breasts mashed against my chest and I moaned, diving back into her mouth to tangle my tongue with hers.

I felt like my dick was a fucking rocket, it was so ready to lift off.

The next thing I knew the ride had stopped and a crowd of people were staring at us. I guess we didn't notice. I wanted the ride to go on and on. As it was I had to hold my jacket in front of me as I climbed out.

I glanced at Frannie. Her pretty lips were swollen and pouting. I wanted to get horizontal with her right fucking now.

Jesus Christ, what was she doing to me?

The girl had the moves that was for fucking sure.

I took her hand and pulled her toward the boardwalk, desperately looking for a place to be alone with her. She smiled at me shyly. There was an innocence in her gaze that made me absolutely sure that she had no fucking clue what I had in mind.

I had a sinking feeling that Frannie was a good girl. That her innocence might be a problem. That it might take more than a Ferris wheel ride to get into her pants. It wasn't going to stop me from trying though.

I knew something else too.

I knew it without a doubt.

This girl was going to be mine.

STOP!

We hope you enjoyed this book and your free excerpts. Please do NOT go back to the beginning of this book before closing it. If you do, the book will not count as being read and the author will not be credited.

Please use the TOC (located in the upper left hand of your screen) to navigate this book. If you're zoomed out, please tap the center of the screen to ensure you are out of page flip mode.

This is true for all authors enrolled in Kindle Unlimited and as such, this message will appear in all of our books that are enrolled in Kindle Unlimited.

Thank you so much for understanding,

Pincushion Press

Made in the USA
San Bernardino, CA
10 March 2018